wicked winemakers

CENTRAL COAST
FIRST LABEL
–BOOK TWO–

RIDGE'S
Release

USA TODAY BESTSELLING AUTHOR

HEATHER SLADE

A complete list of Heather Slade's
series and titles is available at
the end of this book or
visit her website:
HEATHERSLADE.COM

Table of Contents

1

Seraphina

Los Caballeros. There was no proof the secret society even existed, yet my boss had ordered that I, an
assistant district attorney, head up the task force to take
them down. How many people were on the task force?
One. Me. It would be laughable if my job—my reputa-
tion as a prosecutor—didn't depend on it.

So here I was, poised to go after the most powerful
entities in the wine industry, starting with the Ridge
family. In particular, Noah Ridge, the man I'd asked to
meet me for breakfast.

The family was renowned for wine-making, both
on the Central Coast of California as well as in the
Napa Valley, Sonoma, and Russian River regions.
While their Cabernet Sauvignon and Chardonnay were
acclaimed, their Zinfandel outsold the other two varietals at least five to one. Not the syrupy pink kind, but
the rich, full-bodied red the grape made when used to
its full potential.

The pink stuff was a billion-dollar accident, according to wine-industry lore. Someone at a lesser-known winery forgot about the vat of juice, so the owners decided to put it in a bottle and give it away. At the height of its popularity, the stuff the winery had named "White Zinfandel" sold twenty million cases per year.

Regardless of the money they could've made jumping on the White Zin bandwagon, Ridge never had.

They'd stayed their course, continuing to produce some of the best red wine in the world. By doing so, they'd won endless awards and made billions of dollars without succumbing to the hype, thus maintaining the integrity of the varietal. It was a position I envied. Maintaining integrity, that was.

When I'd interviewed for the position of assistant district attorney with San Luis Obispo County, I knew part of the reason I was invited to do so was my connection to the wine industry.

At one point in my life, I'd wanted to pursue a degree in enology—the science of wine and wine-making. From there, I had two options. Either vinification, aka making the stuff. Or viticulture, aka growing the grapes used to make the stuff.

Instead, I'd charted a different course after my father lost the winery that had been in his family for generations to none other than the Ridges.

While coincidental, it wasn't their fault he'd lost it to them. In fact, Noah's father, Hewitt Ridge, had been generous when he bailed mine out of bankruptcy after his experimentation into "non-traditional" varietals failed catastrophically.

Had the saga ended there, I might've been able to follow my dream of working in the industry myself, but in the years following his bankruptcy, my father began drinking heavily. On a fateful night when I was eighteen years old, he left a bar after being there for several hours and got behind the wheel of his car.

He'd made it within five miles of home when he veered into the opposite lane, causing a head-on collision. The family of four in the other vehicle all died on impact, according to the police report filed on the accident. My father, though, had lingered in a coma for four painfully long years before dying.

During that time, the legal fight between the deceased victims' family and mine resulted in us losing what little we'd had left, including the home where I'd grown up.

The decision to become an attorney had been made out of necessity. Once I started, though, I knew it was what I was meant to do. I loved the law and had taken my oath to uphold it seriously.

Now, though, my boss was pressuring me to dismantle Los Caballeros as well as prosecute the man rumored to be at the secret society's helm—Brix Avila. He knew as well as I did we didn't have any evidence to prove they existed, let alone convict them of illegal activity.

In fact, his continued insistence that I make this task force my top priority started to feel as though I was carrying out a personal vendetta against Brix and the perhaps-mythical Los Caballeros.

"Hey, Mom," I said, answering her call as I left the house.

"Hi, baby. By any chance, have you talked to your sister lately?"

"Not since last week. Why?"

"She, um, hasn't come home."

"What do you mean?"

"It's been a few days."

My baby sister had been missing for a *few days,* and I hadn't heard about it until now?

"When was the last time you saw her?" I asked, trying not to let on that I was about to jump straight into panic mode.

"Two days ago."

I sat down, put my head in my hand, and breathed a sigh of relief. Two wasn't a few. In fact, depending on what time she'd last seen her, it might not be the forty-eight hours required to report someone missing.

Not to mention, at twenty-three, my sister, who was six years younger than me, was an adult. Perhaps it would've been nice of her to inform our mother of her whereabouts. However, that wasn't the relationship the two had.

"What happened, Mom?"

"Nothing."

"What was the last thing the two of you talked about?"

When she hesitated, I knew they'd had an argument.

"Let me put it this way. What did you fight about?"

"It wasn't a fight. I told Luisa I didn't want her to bring Jorge to the house anymore. I don't trust him."

Neither did I, but my mom had to know confessing her feelings to Luisa would backfire.

"She's probably staying with him. I'll give her a call."

"Staying with him, but without taking any of her belongings with her? That makes no sense, Seraphina. Not after two days."

"What do you mean by 'belongings'?"

"Her computer, a toothbrush, anything more than the clothes on her back."

I could see Luisa not caring enough to return home for anything my mother had mentioned, except her computer.

In a little over a month, my sister would graduate with a master's degree in business administration. I had no doubt she had final projects due, along with exams to study for. She wouldn't risk failing her classes now, after six years of hard work. Especially not over a fight with our mom.

"I'll give her a call."

"I've been calling. It goes straight to voicemail."

I didn't bother to explain that would be exactly what happened if my sister had blocked our mother's number.

When my call went straight to voicemail too, I got an uneasy feeling. There was no way Luisa would block me. And, like me, she was a morning person. She wouldn't have her phone turned off at this time of the day.

2

Ridge

From the window by the table, I had a perfect view of the restaurant's entrance as well as the ocean, volatile with today's storms.

I'd arrived early for my meeting with Seraphina Reeve, San Luis Obispo county's new assistant district attorney and the woman hell-bent on bringing an end to Los Caballeros—an organization whose traditions withstood the tests of hundreds of years.

That she knew about the secret entity was a problem in itself. Did she truly, or like so many others, had she heard the rumors but had no confirmation?

Glancing up, I saw her walk through the front door, the look on her face as angry as the sea. Or was it troubled?

"Noah," she said, pulling out the chair on the opposite side of the table I'd chosen. "Not surprised you arrived before me." She, too, was early.

I waited for her to get settled. After she had, I still didn't speak. She'd asked for this meeting, and I'd let her show her hand before I did mine.

"I see. Well, this is a waste of time," she muttered when I didn't offer up as much as a hello.

"Why did you ask for this meeting, Sera?"

Yeah, when we talked on the phone the first time and I used the nickname, she'd vehemently told me not to call her that. However, I'd also told her every-one called me Ridge—*not* Noah—yet she insisted on doing so.

"As you know, your *club* has operated outside the law for years. I'm here with an offer."

I raised a brow and waited.

"Brix Avila pleads guilty to several counts of obstruction of justice, and that will be the end of it. Along with proof you've disbanded. If you or anyone else is found guilty of interfering with a single other investigation, we'll prosecute to the full extent of the law."

I took a minute to process the words she'd just vom-ited and did exactly what Brix would've done in my place. I sat back in my chair and laughed. Hard. Then signaled Barb, the waitress who usually waited on me.

"Check, please."

I shook my head as I left, rushing to my truck once I was outside. The storm was picking up, and soon, there'd be a downpour.

My *club*, as Seraphina called it, had been in existence since the fourteen hundreds. A junior prosecutor working for a central California coastal county was hardly a match for us. No matter how beguiling she was.

"If I have to, I'll subpoena Addison Reagan and her mother," said the woman, who'd followed me out to the parking lot. "Maybe then Brix will listen to reason."

The woman she was referring to, Addison Reagan, had been charged with a murder both Seraphina and I knew she didn't commit. I didn't bother to tell her that by the time either woman received as much as a summons, the murder charges against her would be dropped. She'd find out soon enough on her own. Not that it was what she'd subpoena her for. No, it was Los Caballeros' involvement in finding the real killer the ADA would question Addy about. Neither Brix nor any of the rest of Los Caballeros would ever allow that to happen.

I opened the driver's-side door and was in my truck, about to shut it and drive away, when I heard her say, "Wait. Please."

Her two simple words would have been easy to ignore if I hadn't heard the tone in which they were uttered.

"What?" I said, not looking at her.

"There's another reason I wanted to talk to you."

"Not interested, Ms. Reeve."

"But—"

"If you'd led with something other than an idle threat, Sera, maybe then I would've listened." I slammed the door shut, started the engine, and drove away, wishing I could stop myself from glancing in the rearview mirror at the woman still standing in the rain, looking as though she was about to cry.

After driving far enough away that she couldn't see me, I pulled over, dug out my cell phone, and sent a text to the man who had been my best friend since we were both in elementary school. Hard to believe that was thirty years ago.

Call me ASAP, read the group text I sent to Brix and the San Luis Obispo County sheriff, Conrad Krouse, a man everyone called Vader. He'd been given the nickname of the *Star Wars* character because of how loud his breathing sounded on the other end of a phone call.

Since I knew they were currently on a private plane, returning from Alamos, Mexico, I wasn't sure when they might have a signal. I put the truck in gear and took the back roads south to where my new house was being built.

When I'd purchased the property on See Canyon Road and walked the land to find a building site that would take advantage of the sweeping ocean views, I envisioned living there with the woman I'd planned to ask to marry me.

Instead, Alex—Brix's younger sister—had married someone else. In hindsight, thinking I had a shot with her had been naive at best. Stupid was more accurate. Alex and Maddox, her now-husband, had been together off and on since high school. Brix had warned me pursuing her wasn't the best idea. However, I'd been "in love" with her before she met the man she'd married.

So much water had gone under that bridge; it was long since time I moved on. Finding someone I considered half as appealing as Alex, though, seemed unimaginable. She wasn't only beautiful and sexy; she was also smart and funny.

My cell rang, yanking me out of yet another round of lamenting her loss.

"Hey, Brix," I said after swiping the screen to accept his call.

"Ridge, I've got Vader here with me."

"Listen, this new prosecutor is becoming a huge pain in the ass. She's threatening to subpoena both Addy and her mom." I decided to lead with that rather than her threat against Brix and Los Caballeros.

"Why? They're in the clear. Why is she contacting you anyway? Zin is Addison's attorney."

I'd wondered that myself, but maybe I was the only one who'd answered my phone.

"I'll get in touch with her," offered Vader. "She should be working *with* me, not around me."

"Her name is Seraphina—"

"Yeah, Ridge, I know."

When Brix asked what progress was being made in tracking down the person we believed was responsible for the murder Addison had been charged with, it reminded me there were other things I needed to deal with this morning rather than check the progress on my house.

"When will you be back?" I asked after telling him the little I knew.

"About an hour. Maybe less. By the way, Alex called to say the ball is back on for next weekend."

I'd forgotten all about the annual fundraiser benefiting the children's hospital in San Luis Obispo. A couple of years back, Alex had taken over the event, whose biggest moneymaker was a bachelor auction. One that, in a moment of weakness, I'd agreed to participate in.

"Shit," I muttered under my breath.

Brix laughed. "I hear you, buddy."

Easy for him to find it humorous since he already knew who would cast the winning bid for a date with him. Brix had convinced Alex he'd make a sizable donation on top of paying the bid amount himself as long as she agreed to let Addison win. While he hadn't been infatuated with her for as long as I had been his sister, it had moved beyond that now. I had little doubt once they returned to the States, he would ask Addy to marry him if he hadn't already.

As for me, I didn't know exactly who would bid on a onetime date with me, but I predicted it would be a nameless, faceless daughter of one of the area's winery owners. Someone I'd known most of my life, given I was the son of the same, and whom I already knew I had so little interest in. Getting through the evening I had to spend with her would be agony.

3

Seraphina

"That went well," I said out loud, rolling my eyes as I watched Noah Ridge drive away.

I'd certainly made a mess of trying to get the help I was beginning to sense I'd need. Of the two ways I could've approached him, I'd chosen pissed off and argumentative, bluffing that I had enough evidence to arrest his best friend.

Maybe if I'd started by explaining I was worried about my sister. the conversation would have gone differently. Not ending with him stalking out of the restaurant before we'd had the chance to order, or driving away, leaving me standing in an empty parking lot in the pouring rain.

I regretted my conversation with Noah more after another two days passed without a word from my sister.

Neither my mom nor I had been able to reach her. I'd gone so far as to show up at the university, only to be told she'd emailed at least one of her professors, saying she was leaving town and wouldn't be finishing the semester.

With only a month left until graduation? She'd never do such a thing. Something else was going on here, and the more time passed without us hearing from her, the more frightened I became.

While the police had let my mother and I file a missing-persons report, that my sister sent her professor an email saying she'd left town was evidence enough for them that she wasn't *missing*.

My argument that she wouldn't quit school so close to graduation hadn't swayed their belief we were wasting their time at all.

I didn't know much about Luisa's boyfriend, Jorge, including his last name. In a city where twenty percent of its population was Hispanic, I could hardly walk around asking if anyone knew someone who went by Jorge.

My gut told me something was wrong. Really wrong, and when it came to a missing person, time mattered.

I knew my best option to get the help I needed to look for her was to swallow my pride and contact Noah. If Los Caballeros truly did exist, maybe I could convince them to help me look for her, even if it meant paying them.

I didn't have a lot of money saved, but I had ten grand set aside toward a down payment on a house. I had a long way to go, but I made decent income, working for the DA. If I had to use my savings to find Luisa, I would.

I called Noah, not surprised when he didn't pick up. I left a message, saying it was urgent I speak with him, but after several hours, he hadn't returned my call.

I'd also called Zin Oliver, a local attorney and good friend of Noah's who was also rumored to be connected to Los Caballeros. I left a voicemail for him too.

Finally, after not hearing back from either Noah or Zin, I called the sheriff.

"Ms. Reeve, I was headed out the door."

"I won't keep you. I'm trying to reach Noah Ridge on an urgent matter. I've left messages, but he hasn't returned my call."

"My guess is he's already at the Wicked Winemakers' Ball, where I'm also headed."

"If you see him, can you please relay the message that it's imperative I speak with him?"

"If this is about Addison Reagan—"

"It isn't. It's not about her or her mother or Brix or Los Caballeros." I took a breath. "If you see him, would you please reiterate what I said?"

"If I see him."

The call ended abruptly, as did my hope Sheriff Krouse would tell Noah he'd spoken to me.

I opened my laptop and searched for the fundraiser he'd mentioned, then clicked on the page to purchase tickets, knowing if it was sold out, I'd still go. That's how desperate I was to talk to Noah.

When I clicked the button to purchase entry to the event and chose a single ticket, another tab immediately opened, asking for payment.

First hurdle, crossed. Now, what in God's name would I wear to a black-tie event? I rummaged through my closet and found a maxi-length black dress that was far too informal for the ball, but at least, it was long.

After putting my hair in an updo and makeup on, I grabbed a pair of black heels and raced out the door. If I arrived too late for the bachelor auction, at least the hundred dollars I'd spent on the ticket would go to charity.

4

Ridge

"Don't look now, but the ADA just walked in," said Vader. "I wasn't going to tell you this, but since she's here, I better."

"Tell me what?" Was she about to serve us all with subpoenas or something? At a charity fundraiser? God, I wouldn't put it past her. I glanced in the direction Vader had told me not to and saw her looking around the room.

If she was here to serve us papers, she'd certainly gotten dolled up for it. In fact, I'd go so far as to say she looked stunning.

"It's not about Addison, Peg, Brix, or Los Caballeros," I heard Vader say.

"What isn't?"

"I told you. She said it's *imperative* she speak with you and it isn't about any of that."

If it wasn't about Addy, Peg, Brix, or Los Cab, then what did she have to talk to me about? I hated to imagine.

"There's your cue."

"What?"

"Clean out your damned ears, Ridge. Alex announced the bachelors should report backstage."

The timing couldn't have been better. Unless I was right about the subpoenas. If she served them while we were on stage, it would be the talk of the Central Coast for the next hundred years.

"Seraphina is here," I said to Brix, who I found waiting behind the stage's curtain.

His eyes scrunched. "The DA?"

"The assistant DA, but yes, her."

"What in the hell is she doing here?" he asked.

"How would I know?"

"You're the only one she seems to talk to."

"Well, we didn't talk about her being here."

Brix stepped forward and peeked out the curtain. "I don't see her."

Fuck. I hoped that didn't mean she was headed our way.

"Wait. There she is. She's talking to Vader and Peg."

"How do they look?" I asked.

"Vader and Peg?"

"All of them."

Brix shrugged. "Nice, I guess. I don't really pay attention to that kind of thing."

"Not what they're wearing! Their faces. Never mind. Move and let me look."

"Their *faces*?" I heard him mutter.

"They're smiling."

"Smiling? Move. Let me see." I pushed Brix out of the way. "Yep, they're smiling. Wanna explain why that's so interesting?"

"I doubt Vader would be smiling if Seraphina were here to serve us all subpoenas."

Brix's eyes opened wide, and he took a step closer. "Tell me you didn't say what I think you said."

"I said I doubt—"

"Yeah, I heard that part. Explain about the subpoenas."

"Shush." You'd think Alex had shouted at us the way Brix and I jumped. "We're holding an auction here, remember?" she snapped.

"We're holding an auction here, remember?" Brix repeated under his breath, mimicking her. He pulled me away from the stage. "Ridge, this is the most important night of my life. Please tell me I'm not about to get served."

"I doubt it, given Vader was smiling. Plus, the small purse she has with her doesn't look big enough to hold several subpoenas."

Brix glared at me. "If the rest of my life didn't hinge on tonight's event, I swear we'd go outside and have this out."

I was aware of what he had planned, given I'd help make the arrangements. "Naughton Butler is on standby with the helicopter. Your bags are already at the resort."

"Thanks, Ridge."

"Tonight will go perfectly for Addy and you."

As long as Seraphina Reeve didn't throw a wrench into his plans. Given how anxious he already was, I didn't say that. I'd already said too much.

Brix and I were the last two bachelors to go on stage. "Wish me luck," I said when the bidding for the last one before me, Press, ended.

"What do you need luck for?"

"So Baron Van Orr's daughter doesn't bid on me."

Brix nodded in understanding. Of all the "wine-makers' daughters" here tonight, she was the most annoying. Her sense of entitlement had no limit, particularly since Brix's winery and my family's were considerably more successful than her father's.

"You should've rigged it like I did."

"Who would I have made that arrangement with?" Since the only person I'd actually want to bid on me was his married sister, I was interested to see if he could come up with anyone.

"I don't know. How about the ADA?"

"You're hysterical."

"Our next bachelor is Noah Ridge. If you're the lucky winner of a date with Ridge, you'll be treated to both adventure and romance. Your afternoon will start with riding dune buggies on Pismo Beach, followed by a two-person kayak ride in Avila Bay after a hot-air balloon carries you from one beach to the other. Finally, the *coup de grâce* will be a private dinner in the Ridge Winery caves. Who wants to start our bidding?"

To my chagrin, it was none other than Isabel Van Orr, who bid a thousand dollars. I couldn't see the woman who raised it by five hundred. Damn, if things didn't pick up, my date would be the lowest bid of the night.

"Two thousand," countered Isabel.

Justine Norman raised her paddle. "Three thousand."

"Come on, ladies, this is for the kids. Surely, a date with the Central Coast's *second* most eligible bachelor is worth more than three grand."

"Four," said Isabel.

"Forty-five hundred," said someone else I didn't recognize.

"Five," bid Justine.

"I'm out," I heard Isabel say and breathed a sigh of relief. At least, it had gotten as high as it did last year, and I wouldn't be forced to spend another painful evening with Isabel.

"Six," I heard the same woman I hadn't been able to see earlier call out. Her voice sounded vaguely familiar, but since I'd known everyone in the room most of my life, many of them would.

"Seven." The bid came from another person I couldn't see from where I stood.

"Eight."

Justine's paddle went up. "Nine."

"Ten," came the voice from the left side of the room. I tried to see who it was, but without bending at the waist or standing on my tiptoes, both of which would make me look pathetic, my view was blocked.

"Eleven thousand, anyone?" Alex waited a few seconds, but no paddles were raised or bids called out. "Ten thousand, going once, going twice. Sold to our lovely bidder!"

Since Alex knew everyone in the room as well as I did, that she didn't say the winner's name was curious.

"Please stand so our auction assistant can find you," she said, shielding her eyes from the bright light. "Who *is* that?" she asked me after turning off her mic.

I could hear Brix chuckling behind me. "That's the assistant district attorney," he told his sister.

"I don't recognize her. What's her name?"

"Seraphina Reeve," I mumbled, wondering what in the hell the woman was up to now.

5

Seraphina

I'd really hoped it wouldn't take every penny of my savings to win the date with Noah Ridge. Not that I cared about a dune-buggy ride or dinner at his family's winery. No, as soon as we were able to talk in private, I would tell him what I really wanted, and that was help finding my sister.

If ten thousand wasn't enough, I wasn't sure what I'd do. Maybe he'd at least point me in the right direction to start looking for her. Or maybe he'd be able to convince the sheriff to help. One thing I knew without question; Noah wouldn't turn me down flat. He wasn't the type in the same way his father hadn't taken advantage of my family when the opportunity presented itself.

When Samantha Marquez, someone I'd interviewed when Addison Reagan was mysteriously unavailable to meet with me, approached the table and motioned for me to follow, I walked in the direction she had. I didn't bother saying goodbye to the other two people at our nearly empty table since they hadn't said a word to me when I was seated.

"I only need to confirm your bank account information," Sam said once we were a good distance away from the other guests.

"Of course," I said, taking out the checkbook I'd brought with me. "Do you want me to write it out now?"

"A check? No, we don't do any of that here. You'll receive a request from the foundation to wire the funds, along with instructions as to where to send it."

I felt foolish for asking, but I certainly had no idea how these things worked. Sam, though, seemed sympathetic.

"After the lines became impossibly long following the silent auction two years ago, Alex decided it would be much easier for everyone to handle payment this way," she said as she entered my bank account information on an electronic tablet. "And here's your date now."

Sam smiled, but when I turned around to face Noah, he appeared angry. "Are you finished?" he asked Sam.

When she nodded, wide-eyed, he took my arm and led me toward the door.

"What are you doing?" I gasped.

"You first. What in the hell are you up to, Seraphina? And don't think for a minute you'll get away with it. By the way, I'll cover the cost of your bid since I have no intention of honoring the date and I'd hate for the charity to lose out because you were the winning bidder."

As hard as I tried to blink them away, tears spilled onto my cheeks. "I had no intention of going on a date with you, either." His hand still gripped my arm, so I wrenched it away and stormed off in the direction of my car. Not that I could remember where I'd parked or see where I was walking through my tears.

What hurt the most was that I had been so wrong about him. His reaction was the last thing I'd expected. My tears, though, were for my sister and the powerlessness I felt, realizing I had no idea what to do next to find her.

At least I'd still have my ten thousand dollars. Maybe I could use it to hire a decent private investigator.

"Wait," I heard Noah say, but I kept walking, not wanting him to think my tears were because he'd said he wouldn't go through with the date.

I hit my key fob, relieved to see I was only a row away from where I'd parked, when I felt Noah's hand on my arm again.

"Let go of me," I screeched, attempting to wrench away a second time. However, he was better prepared and held on tight.

"Wait. I'm sorry, okay?"

"*Not* okay. Now, let me go."

"It was unexpected. Particularly after your threat the other day."

"Yeah, well, now, it's over. Go back to your party, Noah, and leave me the fuck alone."

He spun me around to face him. "Why did you say you had no intention of going on the date, either?"

"It doesn't matter."

His grip on my arm loosened, but he didn't let go. "It does. Tell me."

I looked up at the night sky, knowing if I refused, I'd be blowing what could be my last chance to get his help. If my sister weren't missing, there would be no way I could swallow my pride. However, I couldn't put myself before her. I'd never been able to, but now especially.

"My sister is missing," I blurted.

"I see."

"I bid on the date because you wouldn't return my calls. No one would. At least Sheriff Krouse answered when I contacted him. He told me you'd probably be here tonight like everyone else. It was my last-ditch effort." I raised my shoulders and wiped my tears. "I can't afford to pay the ten thousand dollars and try to hire someone else to help me, so I appreciate your offer of covering it for me."

"Come with me," he said, moving his grasp from my arm to my hand.

"No! My car is over there." I pointed in the opposite direction.

"And if I let you get to it, you'll drive away before we have a chance to talk."

"Where are you taking me?" I asked when he opened the door of his truck and motioned me inside.

"Somewhere quiet, so you can tell me what happened with your sister."

I folded my arms and refused to get in. "Why?"

He shook his head. "God, you're stubborn."

"*Me?* You won't answer my question."

"If you won't tell me what happened, how am I supposed to help?"

"I can take my own car. If you're really going to listen, I'll meet you."

Noah shook his head. "You're too upset to drive."

"I'm no less upset than I was when I arrived here. Safely, I might add."

"For God's sake, woman." Noah put his hands on my waist, lifted me into the truck, and closed the door. I heard the lock click and was stunned when I couldn't open it.

"Child locks," he said when he got in the other side. "Fitting, since that's how you're behaving."

I opened my mouth to tell him to fuck off, but closed it.

"Good decision," he said, smirking as he started the engine.

It wasn't until he took the turnoff for See Canyon Road that I asked again where we were going. "What are you going to do? Throw me off the mountainside?"

"Yep. You caught on. Rather than letting you drive away, I decided to murder you instead. Knock it off, Seraphina."

I folded my arms and looked out at the moonlight on the ocean. I'd always loved this drive. When I was younger, before Luisa was born, my father would bring my mom and me here. Once we got to the top of the mountain, the views went as far north as Big Sur and south to Santa Barbara. I doubted there was a more beautiful place in all of California.

I was stunned when Noah pulled off the road at the exact spot my father used to.

"I'd suggest we get out and walk, but there's the thing about me murdering you to get past. Not to mention, it's a little too cold for you to be out without a jacket."

"My dad used to bring me here," I said.

"He did? I didn't realize you were from the area."

"Lived here my whole life except for when I was at law school."

"Huh."

I wasn't surprised he hadn't put two and two together with my name. Noah was three years older than I and far more popular. He was probably away at college when my dad lost his birthright. It was doubtful he would've known his father had purchased our family's vineyards and winery operation.

"You said your sister is missing."

I nodded, knowing if I tried to speak now, I'd wind up in tears again.

"Can you tell me what happened?" His voice was soothing, so unlike it had been at the ball.

I took a couple of deep breaths. "My mother called me the day I met you for breakfast. Not that we ate. Anyway, she asked if I've talked to Luisa recently, and when I said I haven't, she told me my sister hasn't been home for two days."

"That was two days ago, so now she's been missing four."

"That's right."

"Is it unusual for her to be out of contact for that length of time?"

"Very. Especially with me. Also, she's about to graduate with a master's degree from Cal Poly. My mother said she left her computer at home."

"I'm guessing any attempts at reaching her have failed?"

"Yes."

"Have you been able to find anything on her computer? What about cell phone use? Bank account or social media activity? Do you know if she's attended any of her classes?"

"None of the above. In fact, I went to the university, looking for her, and one of her professors told me she sent an email, stating she was leaving town and wouldn't be finishing the semester."

"Which doesn't make sense if she's about to graduate. How were her grades?"

"Summa cum laude."

"So quitting with only a few weeks left isn't something she'd do."

"Definitely not."

"Friends?"

"No one has seen or heard from her since last week."

"Does she have a boyfriend?"

I nodded. "His name is Jorge."

"He hasn't seen her, either?"

This was where it became difficult to explain. "She hasn't been seeing him that long. Neither my mother nor I care much for him."

"Have you been able to talk to him?"

"I only know his first name, and I have no idea where he lives."

"Have you had her cell phone tracked?"

"I'd need a warrant."

He raised a brow. "You haven't been able to get one?"

"She's twenty-three and has been missing four days. SLO PD is not exactly seeing this as a priority."

"You couldn't get one on your own?"

"The DA thinks I'm overreacting."

The incredulous look on Noah's face was the same one I'd had on mine yesterday when I approached my boss.

"I need to ask you something."

I'd anticipated he would. The last time we talked, I'd threatened his best friend as well as the very people I was now seeking help from. "I swear I would not lie about my sister being missing in order to trick you into doing something that would jeopardize Los Caballeros—if it truly exists."

He raised a brow and turned his head toward the ocean. "That wasn't what I was going to ask."

"I didn't want you to think—"

"I wouldn't have."

"I'm sorry. What were you going to say?"

"Given your sister's stellar academic career, this seems unlikely, but do you think there's any chance the boyfriend could've talked her into going away?"

"I don't think so, but she is twenty-three."

"Like I said, from the little you've told me about her, it seems unlikely." He turned toward me. "You mentioned your mother hasn't spoken with her. What about your father?"

"He died a few years ago."

"I'm sorry for your loss."

"Thank you." I waited to see if my dad's death would jog his memory. It didn't appear to.

"Tell me about the ten grand. You said you weren't interested in the date."

"It was a spur-of-the-moment decision." Something occurred to me. "Oh my God, I'm such an idiot."

"What are you talking about?"

"The money doesn't go to you; it goes to the charity." So essentially, I'd bid ten thousand dollars to have a conversation with him. I felt sick to my stomach.

"Your plan was to use it to pay me to help you."

I looked away.

"I'm going to help you, Seraphina. And even if you'd offered it to me, I wouldn't have taken your money."

"Why?"

"Am I helping you?"

"Yes."

"Because it's what we do."

"I don't have much money left," I said without looking at him.

"Again, we wouldn't accept your money either way." When Noah covered my hand with his, I glanced over at him. "And I told you I'd cover the cost of your bid."

I shook my head. "You don't have to do that. You said you'd help me. That's all I care about."

"Which, if I'd returned your phone calls, wouldn't have cost your savings."

"I can't let you."

He shrugged. "I'm sure Alex will agree to it if I offer to double the contribution."

"Why would you do that?"

He smiled. "I could let you believe I'm gallant. However, the truth is, I always donate twenty-five thousand to the foundation anyway."

"Thank you, Noah." My eyes filled with tears, and I looked down at his hand resting on mine. I tried to move it away, but he held tighter.

"I promise we'll find your sister."

"How can you be so sure?" I whispered, hating to think what not finding her would mean.

6

Ridge

Some we helped had an inkling the rumor about the secret society was true. Not that we ever confirmed it. Typically, we kept our efforts anonymous.

I could've told her I'd help her and not mention Los Caballeros at all, not that I had by name. However, I had said "we" would help, primarily because the process would be expedited if I didn't have to act as a go-between.

"I don't know how to thank you."

I had a few ideas, beginning with her calling off her dog of a boss. Seraphina wasn't the first ADA he'd used in an effort to prove we existed. Why he would want to made no sense to me. It wasn't like we were stealing from the rich to give to the poor. We were the rich.

While some might find my thinking terribly gauche, I'd say "tough shit." Our ancestors had been helping those in need for hundreds of years.

"You're a good man," I heard her murmur.

"If that's true, which it isn't always, I'm among many."

"It's true."

I shook my head. "A good man wouldn't have left you standing in the pouring rain."

She smiled. "You make a good point. The least you could've done was offer me an umbrella."

"The least I could've done was buy you breakfast and listen to what you had to say."

"I don't want to get into a pissing match over which of us is worse. However, I am the one who threatened to have Brix prosecuted."

"You're right." I winked when her eyes met mine.

"What happens next?"

"I call a meeting, and we get started."

"When?"

I checked the time. The ball would've ended by now, which meant everyone but Brix would be headed home. I dug out my phone and sent a message, asking for anyone available to meet me at the wine caves in an hour.

Less than two minutes later, I'd received confirmation from eight of our ten. I'd included Brix on the message, so he was aware a meeting was taking place, but sent him a private one immediately after, saying he wasn't invited. Not that I believed he'd seen either.

"I need to return you to your car," I said, starting my truck and backing out onto See Canyon Road.

I didn't know Seraphina well, but I found her silence intriguing, especially when we pulled up near where she'd parked and she still hadn't said anything.

"I'll be in touch in the morning."

She appeared to let out a deep breath.

"What?"

"I'm pretty sure my tongue is bleeding."

My eyes opened wide. "Why?"

"From biting it so hard. Do you know how difficult it is for me to stop at two questions?"

I chuckled. "I know exactly how hard it is." I squeezed her hand, then got out to come around and open her door. "We'll talk in the morning. What time do you have to be at your office?"

"Tomorrow is Saturday."

"I knew that." I held out my hand.

"What?"

"Give me your key fob."

Seraphina's eyes scrunched. "Why?"

"I'm going to open your door for you."

"I can do it."

"I know you can. I'll do it anyway."

"Look, this—"

"I'm helping you find your sister, right?"

"Yes."

"Which means I can interrupt you whenever you try to stop me from doing things like opening your door, and you won't argue with me." I waited while she dug out her fob, then held out my hand.

"Good night, Seraphina," I said, giving it back once she was in her car. "Oh, and text me your address."

"You don't already know it?"

"It sounds less creepy if I ask for it anyway."

"I'll send you my mom's address since that's where I'm staying for the time being."

I closed her door and waited for her to pull out before I left as well.

It would take me twenty minutes to get to the wine caves and another ten to reach the room where Los

Caballeros met. Chances were I wouldn't be the first to arrive.

When I entered the room, I saw I was actually last. Two seats at the table were empty—Brix's and Tryst's.

Trystan Avila, Brix's uncle, who was currently seated in the chair I usually occupied, had been Los Caballeros' leader until he stepped down when his wife became ill. Brix had taken his place.

I pointed to the seat reserved for Brix. "Please," I said to Tryst.

He shook his head. "You will lead us tonight, Ridge. Sit in the appropriate chair."

I met the eyes of every man in the room, who nodded before I took my seat. It was the same thing Brix did at the start of every meeting, like Tryst had before him.

"I've asked you to meet me here tonight because someone needs our help. Seraphina Reeve's younger sister, Luisa, is missing, and I've offered our assistance in finding her."

Unlike when I'd asked Seraphina several questions to confirm her sister was, in fact, missing, those in the room waited for me to proceed.

"She was last seen four days ago." I continued to tell them everything I'd learned in the last ninety minutes. "Any questions?" I asked when I reached the end of what I knew.

"You said Ms. Reeve only knows her sister's boyfriend's first name," said Lavery "Press" Barrett, who was seated on Tryst's right and the most "formal speaker" of our members. He was an American but had spent the majority of his youth in England and had acquired an accent I doubted he'd ever let go of.

"Correct."

"Would it be possible for us to obtain a photograph of both him and the missing sister?"

"I'll see what I can find. She said they haven't been together long." I looked around the room when Press didn't say more.

"I'll start tracking her cell phone," said Beau, Press' younger brother, who was also fond of his own British accent.

Tryst was brushing his lip with his little finger. "Do you have a question?" I asked.

He waved his hand. "Not at this time."

I looked over at Press, who was writing notes on his tablet but raised his head. "While Beau is tracking her cell phone and you're obtaining photos, let's begin looking deeper into the sister."

"I'll see if she has any kind of record," volunteered Vaile "Zin" Oliver, the sole attorney in our group.

"I'll check medical records," offered my brother, Dalton, who'd earned the nickname Bones when he became a doctor.

Next, I turned to Salazar and Rascon Avila—aka Snapper and Kick—who were Brix's two youngest brothers. "Please visit the university tomorrow and see if you can find anyone who knows Luisa Reeve or her boyfriend, Jorge."

Both men nodded.

That left Cru Avila, also one of Brix's brothers.

"I'll start checking DMV records. If she doesn't have a car registered in her name, I'll check her mother's. What about her father?" he asked.

"He's deceased," Tryst answered before I could.

"Anything else tonight?" I asked.

When no one spoke up, I adjourned the meeting, saying we'd reconvene tomorrow but I'd let everyone know when and where in the morning.

"Are you releasing anything this month?" Press asked, changing the subject.

"My father wants to wait until December to do a public release. Wine-club members will get shipments of new vintages mid-November. What about you?"

"Something similar. Maybe a few bottles of Pinot." Press seemed distracted, or he was as tired as I was, given it was almost midnight.

"Hey, who won your bid?" I hadn't been paying the slightest bit of attention to who any of the winners were.

Press shook his head. "You don't want to know."

"Which means you have to tell me." I was intrigued when my friend's face flushed. "If you don't, I'll ask the others before they leave."

"My mother."

I raised a brow.

"Both Beau and me. She said it's the only way she can get either of us to spend any time with her."

"Ouch."

"Right? At least she said it privately. Still bloody embarrassing."

"What about the Avila brothers?" I asked.

"Felicity Hope had the winning bid for a date with Cru." As far as winery owners' daughters went, Felicity was one of the least objectionable. "I can't remember who bid on Snapper or Kick."

"Eberly Warwick bid on me," said Snapper, walking over to us.

"Wait a minute. How old is she?" The last time I saw her, she couldn't have been over sixteen.

"Twenty-two or twenty-three. Maybe the same age as Luisa Reeve. I'll ask if she knows her."

"What about you?" I asked Kick, who'd walked up when Snapper did.

"Helena Jordan. She's my mother's age. Maybe older," he grumbled.

"And yet unmarried," said Tryst, also joining us.

"You're welcome to take my place," Kick offered.

Tryst smiled and squeezed his nephew's shoulder. "Perhaps she'll bid on me next year."

I wasn't the only one in the group who raised his eyebrows. "Are you really thinking of being in the auction?" I asked.

"You know Alex. Now that Brix is off the market, she'll need someone to pester."

"But would you do it?" Kick asked.

"Perhaps yes, perhaps no."

"If you'll excuse us, gentlemen," I said when Tryst's eyes met mine. I waited for everyone to leave before I motioned for him to take a seat. "What's on your mind?"

"Are you aware your father purchased Reeve's winery when he almost lost it to bankruptcy?"

I studied Tryst. "Reeve?"

He nodded. "Seraphina's father."

"I had no idea." I knew my dad and the way he did business. I had no reason to think he would've been any less than fair. "How is this relevant?"

"Perhaps you should ask your father."

7

Seraphina

My mother was still awake when I arrived at her house. I hadn't mentioned my plan to ask Noah Ridge for help locating my sister, because I didn't want to get her hopes up.

"Where were you?" she asked.

"I had an errand to run."

"At this hour?"

"I was at the Wicked Winemakers' Ball."

She raised a brow. "You didn't mention you were going."

"It was a last-minute thing. Anyway, I've found someone who is going to help us find Luisa."

Her eyes scrunched. "Who?"

"He's kind of a private investigator who works with other PIs."

"Did you go there to talk to him?"

"Yes. His name is Noah Ridge, and he has experience with this kind of thing."

My mother's face blanched.

"What's wrong?"

"You know the Ridge family purchased the winery."

"Of course I do."

She stood, walked over to the window, and crossed her arms.

"My understanding is the offer he made Dad was very generous."

My mother walked toward the stairs. "Maybe not so generous."

"Where are you going?"

"I'm very tired, Seraphina. We'll talk more in the morning."

If I weren't exhausted myself, I would've insisted she tell me what she meant. However, I could barely keep my eyes open after three almost sleepless nights. I went into Luisa's bedroom and lay down. The apartment she and my mom lived in was small, with only two bedrooms. However, it was bigger than the one I lived in, which was a studio. If Luisa were to come home in the middle of the night, I'd be so overjoyed to see her that I wouldn't mind sleeping on the sofa or even driving home.

I crawled into bed and shut my eyes. Maybe I'd sleep easier tonight, knowing tomorrow I could begin my search for her in earnest.

When I opened my eyes, I was stunned to see it was daylight. More so when I checked the time and saw it was after nine.

I used the bathroom, then went downstairs in search of my mother. While I hadn't let it keep me awake, my mother's statement, "Maybe not so generous," was puzzling. Made more so by her reaction when I'd mentioned Noah's name. She'd gone so pale. On the other hand, could an atypical reaction to anything right now be considered unusual? I had no doubt my responses to Noah were abnormal.

"Mom?" I called out a couple of times, then returned upstairs to see if she was in her room. When I didn't find her there, I went back down the stairs and into the kitchen. I walked over to make a cup of coffee and found a note on the counter near it.

"I've gone to my book-club meeting," the note read.

My mother was in a book club? That wasn't a huge surprise in itself, but my mom told me everything, including which books she was currently reading. Why was I first hearing about a book club now? Not to mention, my sister was missing. It was out of character for her to be so nonchalant. I tried to call her, but it went straight to voicemail.

I went out to the porch and was sipping my coffee when my cell rang. I was about to ask my mother where she really was when I saw the call was from Noah Ridge.

"Good morning," I croaked.

"I didn't wake you, did I?"

"No, I haven't spoken to anyone yet, so my voice is still asleep." I laughed. "Sorry about that."

"It's okay. Listen, do you have time for us to get together?"

"If I didn't, I'd make time. Finding my sister is the only thing I care about."

"Understood. Where are you now?"

"My mom's."

"Where does your sister live?"

"With her."

"I'd like to make arrangements to take a look at Luisa's room."

"Okay." I was about to tell him he could come by anytime, but after my mother's strange reaction the night before, I decided it would be best to check with her first. "That should be fine. My mom isn't here right now, but I'd like to mention it to her before anyone shows up here."

"Again, understood."

I waited for him to say something else, and when he didn't, I thought maybe the call had dropped. "Hello?"

"I'm here."

"Is everything okay?"

"Yeah. I, uh, was about to ask if you wanted to have breakfast. Or lunch."

"But you changed your mind?"

"I wasn't sure if you'd accept the invitation."

"What happened to me not arguing with you since you're helping me find my sister?"

He chuckled. "I'm not going to force you to eat with me, Seraphina."

"You know what I'd really like?"

"I'm afraid to ask."

"Very funny. Anyway, what if I made a picnic and we went back to See Canyon?" I suggested.

"Yeah? I could get behind that."

"What time do you want to meet?"

"I'll pick you up."

"We can meet at my place, then. I need to pick a few things up there anyway."

"When will you be ready?" he asked.

I checked my watch. I needed to shower and maybe swing by the market since I doubted I had much to eat in my apartment. Maybe it would be easier if I picked up food to go. "Um, a couple of hours?"

"Tell you what, if you can swing an hour, I'll bring the picnic. I'm starving."

"In that case, I can be ready in thirty minutes."

"I figured that was what would take the most time. You don't seem like a high-maintenance kind of woman."

"Is that a jab at my outfit last night?"

"What about your outfit? I thought you looked stunning."

I raised a brow, wondering if he was being sarcastic, but it didn't seem like he was.

"Say thank you, Seraphina. It shouldn't render you speechless when I give you a compliment."

"Thank you, Noah. Oh, does it bother you when I call you that? You said everyone else calls you Ridge."

"My mother calls me Noah. And no, I've decided I kind of like it when you do too."

"Do I remind you of your mother?"

"Not in the least. I'll see you in a half hour."

"Wait—oh, never mind."

"What?"

"I was going to give you the address."

He laughed. "Bye, Seraphina."

I left my mother a note, letting her know I'd be gone most of the afternoon but asking her to call me when she got in. Then raced over to my apartment, not remembering what kind of shape I'd left it in last night in my haste to get to the fundraiser. At the very minimum, I knew there were things scattered on my bathroom counter.

While I shouldn't care what Noah thought about my tidiness, I wouldn't want anyone to think I was a slob. One benefit of living in a studio apartment was no matter how bad it was, it wouldn't take me long to straighten it.

It had been less difficult for me to figure out what to wear last night than it was today. The weather was warm for this time of year, but the breeze off the Pacific Ocean was always chilly. Not to mention, the area where we were going was rocky, without a lot of flat surfaces to sit on.

Shortly after I'd finished cleaning up the messes I'd made, I heard a knock.

After checking the peephole, I opened the door. Once I had, I wasn't sure if I should invite Noah in. Was there really any reason to? "Um, ready?" I asked.

"Sure, but you might want to bring a jacket."

"It's right here." I reached over and grabbed it. Noah took a step back, and I locked the door behind me. "Are you sure returning to See Canyon is okay?"

"Absolutely. It's one of my favorite places."

"Mine too."

"On our way, I'll give you an update on the search for your sister."

"Wow. Already? Great."

He ran down the list of things he and his friends, as he'd referred to them, had done so far.

"We were able to get into her cell phone, although her last known location was from the day she disappeared."

"How were you able to get a warrant for her cell phone records so fast?"

He looked over at me. "Probably best if you don't ask about certain things."

"Understood." It was a word he'd used earlier, and it seemed fitting.

"If there's anything I think you should know, I won't hesitate to tell you."

I held up my hand. "Say no more. I will not question your methodologies."

"You know Zin Oliver, right?"

I looked at him with a raised brow.

"Of course you do. For him, sometimes, it's best if he doesn't know certain things, either."

"As an officer of the court."

Noah nodded. "Exactly."

"Got it."

"Two of the guys went by the university, but they'll go back again on Monday when there are more students there."

When he pulled up to the same place he had last night, I saw someone was building a house right below where he'd parked.

"That's a shame," I muttered.

He reached into the backseat and pulled out an actual picnic basket. "What is?"

I waved my arm. "Soon, the view will be gone."

"Not for whoever lives there."

I couldn't justify my reaction, but that what I'd considered "my spot" would soon be gone pissed me off. I was about to say something about how the rich always spoiled everything, but bit my tongue. He was rich and could probably afford to buy property anywhere he wanted to.

"Maybe the owner will invite you over."

I practically snorted. "Fat chance of that," I mumbled.

"Come on. Let's check it out."

He motioned me down the driveway I hadn't been able to see last night.

"We're trespassing."

"It'll be okay."

"But—"

Before I could put my foot in my mouth, so to speak, Noah walked up to the door, entered something into the keypad right above the handle, and it opened.

"*Of course* this is your house," I muttered, feeling like an idiot. It wasn't something I felt often, except when I was around Noah Ridge. I couldn't say why, either.

"I should've said something right away, but I was interested in your reaction."

"So I'd look foolish?" Now, I wished I hadn't suggested a stupid picnic. If we were at a restaurant in town, I could get up and leave like he'd left breakfast.

He set the basket down on the concrete where flooring hadn't been put in yet and took a step closer to me.

"I'd never intentionally do or say something to make you feel foolish, Seraphina."

"Why, then?"

"Honestly? I thought you'd give me some shit about it."

"That's what you were *hoping* for? You're weird." My breath caught when Noah brushed my hair away from my face. His hand felt so big, yet he was so gentle. I remembered when he'd picked me up and put me in his truck last night, thinking he could easily circle my waist with them.

"Your eyes…"

"What about them?" I could barely breathe with him standing so close.

"There's a certain glint you get in them when you're about to give me hell for something."

I took a step backwards. "And you like it? As I said, you're weird." I motioned to the picnic basket. "I thought you were starving."

"I make you uncomfortable," he mumbled, grabbing the basket and carrying it through the open rooms toward a sliding glass door. "I asked the contractor to put the deck on as soon as he could, so I could sit out here."

"It's huge!" I gasped, ignoring his comment about making me uncomfortable. "And the view is even better than from on top."

Something about what I'd said flustered him, and rather than respond, he set the basket on a teak table big enough to seat eight. He opened it and took out sandwiches, salads, fruit, a cheese plate, and cookies. The last thing he removed before plates, cups, napkins, and flatware, were bottles of Italian lemonade and water—still and sparkling.

"What, no wine?" I asked, self-conscious now of whether I had a "glint" in my eye.

"I keep several bottles here if you'd like some."

"I was teasing. given it appears the only possible thing missing."

He smiled.

"Can I help?"

"I got it. You take in the views."

While I knew he meant the ocean, I took in the view of him instead. Noah Ridge was the epitome of a manly man. The reference nearly made me laugh, but it was true. He was tall—well over six feet—with broad shoulders and an equally lean and muscular physique.

His dark hair had streaks in it from the sun and was longer than I'd noticed previously. It hung just past his shoulders. He kept his beard neatly trimmed. In fact, every time I saw him, it looked exactly the same. It had to require daily maintenance, yet he didn't seem like the kind of guy who would care enough to fuss with it.

Today he wore a long-sleeved white shirt and tattered jeans, but the kind that looked like he'd own them long enough for them to fray, not that he'd bought them that way. He had on a pair of black motorcycle boots that appeared equally worn.

"Do you ride?" I asked.

"All the time. My friend Press owns a place with beach access. Not many places like that left."

My eyes scrunched. "You ride on the beach?" I knew it was still legal to drive cars on the dunes at Pismo Beach, but I couldn't remember ever seeing motorcycles. It didn't seem safe.

"There's nothing like the feel of the ocean spray on your face, the wind in your hair, and the horses love running in the tide."

"Horses?"

"What did you think I meant?"

I pointed at his boots. "Motorcycles."

"Oh. No. Unless the sand is really packed, I wouldn't think it would be safe."

I laughed.

"Is that funny?"

"I was thinking the same thing."

"Ready?" he asked, pointing to the bench seat facing the ocean. Once I sat down, he slid in beside me. "I thought you might like to look out at it since you were looking at me before rather than the ocean."

8

Ridge

There was that glint I liked so much. This time, though, instead of frowning, Seraphina smiled.

"You're an interesting character," she said, dishing some of the Greek salad onto her plate. Somehow, I'd known she'd like it.

By her coloring, she could be Greek. Her shoulder-length wavy hair was darker than mine, and her brown eyes turned almost black when she gave me *that* look. In flat shoes, like she was wearing today, she barely came up to my shoulder.

Unlike Alex, whose model-thin body I'd always considered my ideal, Seraphina was curvy. Her breasts would be more than a handful for the average man—something I'd never been. My mother joked I wore size-twelve men's shoes when I came out of the womb. And while her heart-shaped ass was squeezably lush, her waist was tiny. I remembered being surprised at the size of it, last night, when I picked her up and set her on the seat of my truck.

Until today, and last night, I'd only seen her in business attire. She seemed more relaxed while dressed casually. She'd probably sway the opinions of many more jurors if she were able to wear tight jeans to court.

"What are you thinking about?" she asked, bringing a forkful of salad to her lush lips.

"You," I said, reaching over and plucking a Kalamata olive off her plate and popping it into my mouth.

"Elaborate."

"You tell me what you were thinking about earlier when your eyes took in every inch of me, then I'll tell you."

"I was thinking you need a new pair of jeans."

"You were not."

She raised a brow. "You're a mind reader?"

I shook my head and took a big bite of an Italian sub.

Seraphina patted her lips with her napkin, sat up straight, and folded her arms.

"Tell me about Luisa," I said when her expression went from smiling to serious.

"If you think I get a glint in my eye, you should see my sister. She is a force of nature, that one."

"More than you? I find that hard to believe."

She cocked her head and smirked. "Luisa is like a hurricane. She's calm one minute, then raging the next. She and my mom are so much alike."

"Are you more like your dad?"

Seraphina shrugged. "I'm not sure. Maybe at one point in his life. By the time I was old enough to really know him, he'd changed."

"How so?" I took another bite of my sandwich, waiting as she thought about her answer.

"I guess life got the better of him."

"You went into law, and your sister business?"

"One lawyer in the family is enough." She set her fork on her plate. "Have you been able to find anything about her boyfriend?"

"Not yet." That wasn't exactly true. What little we had found was curious, bordering on troubling.

Beau had hacked into Luisa's cell phone records, and the number we guessed belonged to Jorge was no longer working. When he took a deeper look, he found it was a burner phone. Then, when he tracked where she'd been, the house we guessed Jorge had lived in was vacant. The other troubling thing was, the last activity on Luisa's phone was from the morning she'd gone missing. Last known location—the vacant house.

Given they were more likely to get answers from neighbors than he was, Beau asked Snapper and Kick to see what they could find out.

While they looked almost like twins, two years separated the brothers, who were champion team-ropers who competed on the PRCA—Professional Rodeo Cowboys Association—circuit. Having spent so much time at their uncle's ranch in Mexico when they were growing up, both spoke fluent Spanish, like most of the residents in the neighborhood surrounding the vacant house.

"How many languages does your sister speak?"

"One. If you're asking if she speaks Spanish, the answer is no."

"Tell me about her boyfriend."

"To me, he looked like a thug. Albeit a handsome one. Suave too, the handful of times I met him."

"Mexican?"

"At least in descent would be my guess, based on his first name, although he didn't speak with an accent."

"Type of clothes? Car he drove?"

"Clothes weren't anything out of the ordinary. The jeans, shirt, and boots he had on the last time I saw him looked a lot like what you're wearing now. As far as his car, it was a white truck, American-made. Maybe a Ford."

"Did she say where she met him?"

"Only that she was out for dinner with friends." Seraphina turned to face me. "You know something about him you're not telling me."

"We believe he had a burner phone. The location we tracked your sister to is a vacant house."

She put her head in her hands.

"We have people checking with neighbors to see if anyone knew him or knows where he might've gone, who he lived there with. That kind of stuff."

"Are you sure he lived there?" she asked without moving her hands from her face. Her voice sounded shaky.

"Based on what we found in her phone records, she spent a lot of time there."

"This is a fucking nightmare." Now more than shaky, it sounded as though Seraphina was crying. I slid closer on the bench and put my arms around her. When she rested her cheek on my chest, I could feel the dampness from her tears.

"You said she met this guy when she was out for dinner with friends. Do you know whom with? If you do, we'd like to talk to them," I said when she pulled away and wiped her tears.

"I got in touch with them the day my mom told me Luisa hadn't come home. I asked what they knew about him, but like me, all they said was his name was Jorge."

"No one spent time with them together?"

"No one I talked to. I'll put you in contact with them, though. Her best friend's name is Jada Yáñez."

"Yáñez?"

Seraphina nodded. "I think she's related to the Avilas. They met at Cal Poly."

"If it's the same Jada, she's Brix's cousin."

"I wasn't sure."

"When possible, I'd still like to check out her bedroom. It might be better to do it at a time when your mom isn't home, mainly because I don't want to upset her more than she already is."

Something about what I said appeared to worry her, but she nodded. "I'll ask. Would it be you?"

"It can be."

The worried look intensified. "Or I can ask Press or Beau to do it. Or both. Moms usually like them. I think it's the English accent."

Whether it was because I'd smiled or that I said I didn't have to be the one looking through her sister's belongings, her anxiety appeared to lessen a little.

Seraphina stood and walked over to the deck's railing. "I've always believed this is the best view in all the world."

I stood next to her. "I would have to agree. It's why I chose this spot for my house."

She looked up at the second story. "Will you have another deck up there?"

"That's the plan."

"It will be amazing."

"Would you like a tour?"

"Um, sure?"

I held up both hands. "No pressure."

"Do I need a hard hat or anything?"

"I wouldn't let you walk around here if it wasn't safe, Seraphina."

"I know."

I couldn't figure this woman out. One minute, she was looking me up and down like she wanted me for lunch and crying on my shoulder. The next, I felt like she didn't want me rifling through her sister's room—even though I was the person she'd asked to help find her—and she didn't want to see my house.

I'd concede there wasn't anything wrong with her not wanting to look around here. There wasn't much to see. "I guess it's not that exciting."

"I'm sorry. I broke my arm when I was a kid, walking through a part of the winery that was under construction. I get nervous."

"Maybe another time."

"Noah?"

"Do you want any more of this?" I asked, pointing to the food she'd hardly eaten.

Seraphina walked over and put her hand on my arm when I started putting the lids on containers. "Noah? Would you please look at me?"

I stopped, set down the sandwich I was about to wrap, and stared into her brown eyes. "Yeah?"

"I would love to see your house, and I would like more to eat. We started talking about Luisa, and I lost my appetite for a minute. It's back now, and if you put the Italian sub I've been drooling over away, you'll definitely see a glint in my eye."

"Sub or tour first?"

"Oh, that's tough." She picked up the sandwich and took a big bite. "Tour," she said, wiping her mouth with a napkin.

Most women didn't rattle me. Too often, they bored me to tears, not that I was an asshole about it. One woman—Alex Avila-Butler—shook me to my core. I never dreamed I'd meet another. In fact, I'd been certain I wouldn't. Today, I was proven wrong. I would never be bored when I was around Seraphina Reeve, and she sure as hell had me shaking in my boots.

It was four in the afternoon by the time we returned to her apartment.

"Do you want to come in?" she asked, staring at something on her phone.

"Looks like you're busy."

"My mom." She shrugged and put the phone down. "She's acting very strange. I guess that's to be expected with my sister missing."

"She probably isn't getting much sleep."

"Neither of us are."

"I'll go. We can talk tomorrow."

"I was about to open a bottle of wine if you'd like a glass. I promise you'll like it. Although my place is pretty small, I do have a patio where we can sit."

"If you're sure you don't want to call it a day."

"To be honest, last night was the first night I slept straight through. I think it's because knowing you were going to help us was such a relief. In other words, I'd like you to stay for a bit."

"Nice choice," I said when I saw her open a bottle of Los Caballeros Cabernet Sauvignon.

"I'm all out of Ridge."

"It's okay. I prefer Brix's anyway."

"No, you don't, and I really am all out. Look." She pointed to a vase that held wine corks. Many of them bore the Ridge Winery logo.

"What's your favorite?" I asked.

"The Vineyard Twenty-Seven Blend."

I raised a brow. "Not many people know that's one of ours."

She shrugged a shoulder. "I do."

"It's not easy to get, either."

"I know that too." She poured two glasses and handed one to me.

"I may have a bottle or two in my cellar."

"I would never ask you to give it up for me."

"What if we drank it together?"

"It should be a special occasion," she said, leading me out to the small patio.

"We'll drink it with Luisa when we find her."

9

Seraphina

I wasn't lying when I said that particular wine was my favorite. It far and away was. However, once I mentioned it, I'd wondered if he'd make the connection to that vineyard and my family. It didn't appear he had.

My father used to tell me the grapes grown there were magical. "The wine they make will dance on your tongue, Sera," he'd say, plucking a fruit and giving it to me to eat.

It was Ridge's vintners who'd coaxed the magic from those grapes, though, not my father. In fact, my dad's endless experimentation ended up being his downfall. I didn't remember those days well, but I did recall one conversation between my parents. I was sixteen at the time and had come downstairs for a bowl of cereal before bed.

"You're obsessed with it," I'd heard my mother say. "To the exclusion of everything else. Me. The girls. All you care about is that damned vineyard. I hate that plot of land."

I'd raced back upstairs, not wanting to hear another word. My mom knew what she'd said would hurt him, and she'd done it anyway.

I realized Noah was studying me. "What are you thinking about?" he asked.

"My parents. My father mainly."

"I don't know what I'd do if I lost my dad." He shook his head. "Sorry, I know that doesn't help."

I held out my glass, and we toasted. "That's a really good thing, Ridge. Not everyone can say they're close to their parents."

He took a drink. "Ridge, huh?"

"I know it bugs you when I call you Noah."

"I told you earlier it didn't."

"You were being nice."

"You don't know me very well if you think I'd do something only to be nice."

He winked and I smiled.

"I'll stop calling you Sera if it bothers you."

"It's what my dad called me. He was the only one who ever did."

He took a sip and studied the wine in his glass. "My mother calls me Noah; your dad called you Sera. It's interesting, isn't it?"

"You know how you said it doesn't bother you?"

"I swear it doesn't."

"It doesn't bother me, either."

"And if I call you Seraphina?"

"It won't bother me either way." I set my glass down, knowing as much as I might want to stay right here and talk to Noah as late as he'd stay, I couldn't. I had to get over to my mother's, and to do so, I couldn't drink any more wine.

"I should probably be on my way," Noah said, perhaps noticing I hadn't taken another sip for several minutes.

"Me too." I still needed to talk to my mom about someone looking through Luisa's room. It wasn't a conversation I looked forward to having. "I'll call you tomorrow about my sister's room."

"You understand we'd be looking for clues as to who her boyfriend is or anything else that might help us figure out where she might be?"

"I do."

I walked him to the door and thanked him for lunch and what ended up being dinner too since he'd insisted on sharing half of what was left with me.

When I arrived at my mom's apartment, she was in the living room, watching television. She didn't turn it down or get up like she always did when my sister or I came home.

"Mom?"

"What, Sera?" My shoulders tightened. She also never called me anything other than Seraphina. More often, she called both Luisa and me "baby."

"We need to talk."

"Maybe in the morning."

"No. Tonight." I walked over, picked up the remote, and turned the television off. "There are things we need to discuss."

"Such as?"

I sat on the sofa, next to her. "Don't you want to know what progress has been made with our search for Luisa?"

"Of course I do."

"Then, why—never mind. Look, we also need to talk about Noah Ridge." She tried to stand, but I grabbed her arm. "Mom?"

"We can talk about Luisa, but I have no interest in discussing the Ridge family."

"It's the same conversation. Noah is helping us. I don't understand where this attitude is coming from. You were the one who said the deal they gave Dad on the winery was a good one."

"I told you I'm not talking about it tonight."

"We have to. Noah will be here tomorrow."

"Why?"

"He wants to look through Luisa's room."

"No."

When she wiggled her arm from my grasp, I stood and followed her into the kitchen. "Mom? Explain this to me."

"I don't want anyone going through her room."

"What if it resulted in them finding something that, in turn, helps them find her?"

She shook her head.

"Tell me what you have against the Ridges. Right now."

"They stole something from your father."

"What? Wait. As I said, *you* told me the deal they gave Dad was fair."

"This was later."

"Later when?"

"The night…*it* happened, Hewitt Ridge took your father's formulas."

"What are you talking about?"

"You know how your father was. He didn't believe in computers. Everything was handwritten. Hewitt stole them."

"Stole what?"

"The formulas for the wines he was developing."

"What would Hewitt Ridge want with them?" Those experiments cost us the winery, as my mother well knew.

"One was for Vineyard Twenty-Seven."

"Okay. I still don't—"

"It was your *father's* blend. It *is* your father's blend."

"Mom, you can't prove that."

"Can't I?"

"How would you? You said the formulas were handwritten. If you were able to determine the wine's composition, you still wouldn't know if it matched what Dad was experimenting with, since they're no longer in your possession."

"I've tasted it."

This conversation was ridiculous. If my father had possessed the same formula Ridge now used, why had his wine been such a spectacular failure versus the success Noah's family now had with it? My mother wasn't making any sense.

"The night of the accident, your father found out Hewitt was at the bar. He went there to confront him, to get back what belonged to him. Hewitt refused."

"Wait. If it was the night of the accident, how do you know he refused? Dad never woke from the coma."

"I just do."

Maybe the lack of sleep was getting to her. Rather than antagonize her further, I backed off. "What if someone else came and looked in Luisa's room?"

"Who?"

"The Barretts—Press and Beau." God, I was so stressed by this conversation I couldn't remember Press' real name. "Lavery!" Thank goodness I remembered. It would've driven me crazy if I hadn't. "Lavery and Beau Barrett."

"That would be fine."

"I'll let them know, and when I find out when they'll be here, I'll let you know too."

"I'm going to bed."

"Good night, Mom."

"Good night, baby."

My mother's behavior baffled me, but thankfully, she'd agreed to let *someone* search Luisa's room. I pulled the cork out of the bottle of wine I'd brought from my apartment and poured a glass, wishing I was drinking it with Noah rather than alone in my mother's kitchen.

I picked my phone up and sent him a text, saying his idea about having Press or Beau search my sister's room was a good one. I also asked him to let me know when he thought they might arrive. There were marching dots on the screen before I set the phone down.

That works. Let me know how early they can arrive.

Eight? I responded.

That early on a Sunday? How about ten?

I shook my head and chuckled. *That's fine.*

Tell me, Sera. Will you be up that early?

I'm an early bird. Except for today when I'd slept until nine.

I am too.

But eight is too early?

For Beau, it is. Press not so much.

I had a nice afternoon. Sounds weird to say with my sister missing.

You can still have nice afternoons.

Thanks, Noah.

Good night, Sera.

Good night.

I wished he hadn't said good night so quickly. On the other hand, there was nothing else to chat about. Still, I felt oddly lonely as I finished the small amount of wine I'd poured, turned off the downstairs lamp, and went up to Luisa's room.

There was no light shining from my mother's bedroom door, not that I would've gone in to talk to her if there had been.

I changed into my pajamas, washed my face, brushed my teeth, and crawled into the full-size bed. It took up most of the space in the small room that otherwise held a desk, one bookshelf, a dresser, and a nightstand. I wondered if I should tell Noah only one person would be needed to search her room. Two men the size of Press and Beau wouldn't fit in here at the same time.

I picked up my phone to send a text, decided I could do it in the morning, and was about to set it down when I saw another message from him.

Still awake?

Yes.

I had a nice afternoon too. And evening.

Me too.

I could've kept talking to you.

Same.

I'll let you get to sleep.

I smiled. *I'm not tired.*

Me neither.

I like your house.

The dots marched, then stopped, then started again, then stopped again. This went on for a couple of minutes.

Everything okay? I asked.

Yeah. Sorry. I...

That was weird. *I what?*

You said you liked my house.

I do. So?

I like you.

10

Ridge

I watched the screen, holding my breath and waiting for Seraphina to respond. Finally, I couldn't hold it any longer. Before, I could tell when she was typing a response. Now? Nothing. Maybe she hadn't seen it yet.

I got out of bed and walked into the hallway, only to turn around and grab my phone from where I'd tossed it on the dresser. Here I was, a thirty-eight-year-old man, and I felt more like a thirteen-year-old.

Gah. Maybe I should try to recall it. But what if she'd seen it already? Then it would be weird. She'd told me twice today I was.

I went downstairs, opened the fridge, grabbed the carton of milk, and took a swig. I remembered there were a couple of cookies left from the picnic, so instead of taking another drink from the carton, I poured a glass, found the cookies, and stood by the kitchen window, telling myself I wouldn't look at my phone again until I'd eaten them. I only made it through half of one before my resolve gave out and I picked up my phone.

Still nothing. *Shit.* Why hadn't I trusted my first instinct and not sent it? Her sister was missing. We weren't dating, for God's sake. She was probably freaking out right now, not knowing how to respond.

Finally, I saw the dots on the screen, indicating she was typing something.

Sorry. My mom was having a nightmare. I like you too.

I downed the milk, shoved the rest of the cookie in my mouth, and turned off my phone so I wouldn't be tempted to say something else stupid. My resolve lasted less than thirty seconds. I couldn't turn my phone off. What if something happened and Seraphina needed to reach me? Or someone else? Like my parents. Or my brother. Or Brix. Or any Los Caballeros.

Are you still there?

Shit. Now, what was I supposed to say? Glad you like me too? Especially given I'd reverted to being an adolescent.

Well, good night.

Wait. I ran my hand through my hair, raced upstairs, and got in bed. *How's your mom?*

She's okay. Acting strangely.

She had a good excuse to be. Her daughter was missing. Me? My odd behavior was inexplicable. Except, if I was being honest, at least with myself, there was something about Seraphina Reeve I'd liked the moment I met her.

Another text popped up on the screen. *Like you said, I'm sure she's exhausted.*

Please assure her we're doing everything we can to find your sister.

I will.

I was about to respond when I saw she was typing something else

Will I see you tomorrow? I mean since Press and Beau are the ones coming to the house?

I thought about telling her I could come too, but I sensed she'd turn me down. *We could get together later in the morning if you'd like.* Jesus. She hadn't said she wanted to get together; she'd only asked if she'd see me tomorrow.

I would like.

I smiled. *I would like too.*

After we'd both said good night a second time, I sent a message to Press, letting him know tomorrow at ten was a go, then turned off the light on my bedside table, closed my eyes, and pictured Seraphina standing on the deck of my new house, looking out at the ocean. In my imagination, she turned around and looked me up and down like she had earlier in the day. Had her eyes been full of desire, or was I dreaming it?

I know when I studied her, mine were. It was all I could do not to pull her into my arms and kiss her bee-stung lips, then run one hand over the swell of her breasts while I reached between her legs with the other. The way the property was positioned, the view of my deck was obscured from any other houses, not that there were any close by.

If anyone were watching, it would have to be through a telescope. Binoculars wouldn't be powerful enough for someone to see me strip Seraphina bare, kneel before her, and kiss my way from her breasts to her belly button, then I'd spread her legs—*and her sister was missing*. What was wrong with me?

I rolled out of bed a second time and grabbed my laptop. I logged in to the software Brix had gotten from Laird Butler, the man who owned the winery and vineyards next to the Los Cab property.

Rumor was Laird and his wife, Sorcha, had met years ago when they both worked in intelligence in the

UK. Given their oldest son was at least a couple of years older than me, we were talking way back to the days of the Provisional Irish Republican Army.

Like Brix's parents, Laird and his wife had raised far more kids than my parents had. They'd had two—my brother, Dalton, and me. The Butlers had four boys and two girls, whereas Brix's parents had six boys and one girl. The one girl who used to plague my thoughts daily.

I glanced over at the time and saw it was close to midnight, and this was the first time Alex had popped into my head since this morning. Seraphina Reeve, though, had been on my mind almost constantly. When we were together, it was impossible for me to think straight, let alone think about anyone else.

After I'd left her apartment, I thought about her all the way home, again when I took the leftover food out of my truck and when I ate it, wishing I was still with her. I'd probably dream about her too.

Man, I had it bad, but this time, maybe it wasn't over the wrong woman.

I refocused on my computer and watched as the software scanned every type of social media in existence, including the platforms that had come and were already gone. First, it scoured for names. Then images. Once a confirmed match was made, the software went back and looked for other pages where Luisa Reeve had been mentioned, photos she'd appeared in, or posts where she'd been tagged.

It would take several hours to complete, but by the time I woke in the morning, I would have a completed report, one that would comprise a chronological detail of Luisa's presence on the internet—including things people believed had been deleted.

When Brix first brought the software to our attention, we'd run it on all the current members of Los Caballeros and a few who no longer were—like my father and Brix's.

The coolest thing about it was what the program could do once the report was generated. I'd sat and watched as one click of a mouse methodically went through and deleted every existing piece of information about me. I ran it on myself again two weeks later, and there was nothing to be found, including on the dark web.

I closed my laptop and set it on the bedside table.

I woke with the sunrise the following morning, which at this time of the year wasn't exactly early. If I left the house now, I'd still be able to catch decent-size waves off Pismo Beach Pier. While the water would be cold, at least in October, it hovered close to sixty degrees versus December, when it would dip into the forties.

I pulled into the beach parking lot twenty minutes later, unsurprised to see vehicles I recognized. Press was here. Maybe Beau too. Zin was parked a few spaces down from me but must've arrived recently since he was standing next to his SUV, towel around his waist, putting on his wetsuit.

"Ridge, I wondered if I'd see you here this morning," he said when I walked over.

I looked out at the water. "Who else is here?"

"The usual suspects." He dropped his towel, pulled the cord connected to the back zipper of his neoprene suit, and sat on the tailgate to put on his booties. "I heard Press is headed over to the mother's house later."

"That's right. Oh, and I ran the search-and-eradicator software on Luisa Reeve last night. I'll forward the report to the rest of you later."

"What we've found so far isn't good, man."

"I know."

"Vacant house. Burner phone. Smells like trafficking to me."

It was my first thought as well, and if it was, Luisa could be on the other side of the world by now.

"Suit up. Let's get out there before the groms hit the water with their newly waxed boards—the ones they picked up at the swap meet yesterday." Zin pointed. "Look, there's one now."

The shortie wetsuit was a dead giveaway of a beginner this time of year. The guy Zin pointed to wasn't wearing booties, either. I predicted the kid would be in and out of the water in under fifteen minutes, hands and feet numb, after pissing off at least a dozen old-timers by putting himself in the wrong position for an incoming wave.

"Fucking groms," I heard Zin mutter as he took off down the beach, carrying his longboard over his head. "See ya out there."

We all lasted about an hour since the waves were crap and the water crowded.

"Whose idea was it to show up here on a Sunday?" grumbled Beau, glaring at his older brother.

"You could've stayed in bed, you pussy," Press shot back before turning to me. "Do we have time for breakfast?"

"I told Seraphina you'd be there around ten, so we have an hour."

"I'll get a table." I heard Cru say, who I hadn't realized was here.

"Were you out on the water?" I asked him.

"Nah, I saw the waves were shit, so I didn't bother."

"Smart man."

"That, I am. So, Huck's or Penny's?"

"Huck's," I answered, as did everyone else.

"Why does he bother asking?" said Beau as he pulled a hoodie over his head and stepped into his sandals.

"He's *your* best mate," said Press.

"Sod off," Beau said over his shoulder to his brother as he ran to catch up with Cru.

"Have you heard from Brix?" Zin asked.

"Hell no," I said, laughing.

"Glad to hear it," he muttered.

"Addison is good for him," said Press. "Did you hear he let Cru bring in the rest of the harvest?"

Among our group of friends, Brix was the worst when it came to being a workaholic. Or he had been up until Addy was accused of murder and he'd basically walked away from the winery altogether to help exonerate her. I hoped once they were married—and I had no doubt they would be—he wouldn't go back to working the number of hours he had been.

"Did you hear Tryst gave him a five-thousand-acre parcel of land adjacent to his ranch in Alamos?" Zin asked as we walked to the restaurant.

"I did. Early wedding present."

"I looked. There's no more land for sale down there. Lucky bastard."

I agreed. Tryst's ranch was a magical place I wished I made time to visit more often. While I loved the land I'd bought in See Canyon, if Tryst offered me a trade, I'd take it in a heartbeat. Not that he ever would.

As for working too much, I was probably considered the biggest slacker of our crew. I worked my ass off when I needed to, but I didn't look for something to do during the slow times of year in the wine business. Now was one of them. The growing season was over. Grapes had been harvested and crushed. There might be some bottling to do, but it would be sporadic. My plan had been to use the time to help get my house finished.

Now, most of my attention was focused on finding Luisa Reeve. And on Seraphina. *Mostly* on Seraphina.

I was a man obsessed, and considering it was for the second time in my life, I wondered if I should talk to someone about it. Not Brix. He deserved uninterrupted time with Addy. I wasn't sure my dad was the best option either. Or my brother.

Later, once we'd finished breakfast, I'd call Tryst. While he was Brix's uncle, he'd always been a surrogate to me too.

"Where'd you go?" Zin asked, nudging me. "I ordered you a coffee since Barb couldn't get your attention."

"Sorry." I shook my head and studied the menu, although I already knew what I'd order. As soon as Cru mentioned Huck's, I'd been craving their Cajun omelet. It was packed with andouille sausage, shrimp, onions, and peppers, then topped with Creole sauce.

I wondered if Seraphina liked Cajun food. *"Shit,"* I said under my breath.

"What?" Zin asked.

I shook my head a second time. "Seraphina Reeve."

"What about her?"

I lowered my voice, not wanting everyone else at the table to hear me. "I spent yesterday afternoon with her."

"She's hot. I'll give you that. Kind of a bitch, though. And what was the deal with her bidding on you at the bachelor auction?"

"She wanted to get me to help find her sister."

"Why didn't she just ask?"

"Because I wouldn't return her phone calls."

"You probably had a good reason."

"She threatened to prosecute Brix if Los Caballeros didn't disband."

I expected a different reaction from Zin when he sighed and sat back in his chair. "Not the first time William Cooley tries to sic someone on us. Won't be the last either, unless he gets voted out. Which, by the way, I don't see happening any time soon."

"Why's he got such a hard-on about us?"

Zin chuckled. "Cause we get away with shit. He sees himself as the lawman in these here parts, and he don't like no vigilantes showin' him up."

I laughed at Zin's "old west" schtick. "She's backing off."

"Hell, I'd hope so. It would suck pretty bad if we found her sister and she used it against us."

"She wouldn't do that."

Zin studied me. "I didn't say she would. Man, you've got it bad. About time."

I didn't need to ask what he meant. There wasn't a person who knew me who didn't think it was time I moved on from Alex.

After breakfast, Press and Beau left for Seraphina's mother's apartment, and I went home to review the report I'd generated overnight. When I opened the document and skimmed it, I found an article pertaining to both her and her sister.

"Drunk driver kills family of four," the headline read. According to the article, Joseph Reeve was found to have a blood alcohol level twice the legal limit when his car veered into the opposite lane and struck another vehicle. The names of all four victims were listed, two of whom were children.

Reeve had survived but was hospitalized with critical injuries. Farther down in the report was another article, much shorter and from almost four years after the accident. It stated Joseph Reeve had passed away from "natural causes" after remaining in a coma since the night of the accident.

Seraphina's comment, "I guess life got the better of him," played over in my head. Alcoholism was prevalent in any industry whose main focus was the creation, sale, or service of liquor, including the wine business. It was especially true with my grandfather's generation.

As a result of what he'd experienced growing up with not one but two parents who overindulged, my own father insisted my brother and I learn how to consume alcohol responsibly—especially in the winery, where it was easy to have what amounted to glass after glass when tasting vintages to determine when to bottle. The reason there were rows of drains in any storage area, whether for barrels or bottles, was as much to allow the winemakers to spit after they tasted as it was to prevent flooding.

Given Seraphina's father's BAC the night of the accident, it was hard to imagine he wasn't an addict. Most people would've passed out at the level stated.

The report mentioned other articles as well as information pulled from court documents over the legal troubles the family had following the incident. Including their home going into foreclosure.

While I didn't know the details of my father's purchase of the Reeve Estate, I was surprised to learn the house wasn't part of the transaction. I was more surprised my father hadn't stepped in to purchase it when the family lost it. At the very minimum, I could see him allowing Mrs. Reeve, whose first name was Leah, and her two daughters to continue living in it.

I'd call my dad and ask, but like me, he was taking much-needed time off after the busiest part of our year. He and my mother were in Australia, visiting their closest friends, the Cullens, who owned one of the oldest privately held wineries on the west coast of Australia. Any questions I had about what had happened with Joseph Reeve could wait until they returned.

There were several pages of photos included, but as I scrolled through them, I saw none of Luisa with anyone who appeared to be a boyfriend. In fact, almost none of them were of her with men at all. In the few there were, everyone had been identified and none were named Jorge or anything close. I zoomed in on the images and took a second look.

About halfway through the bunch, there was a photo of Luisa with four other women. They were in the bar of a restaurant I recognized. It was in downtown San

Luis Obispo, and the date the photo was posted was earlier this year.

I zoomed in again and examined the image in greater detail. In the background, two men were looking in the direction of the four women. They appeared to be studying more than admiring them. Zooming in further resulted in too much pixelization, so I decreased the amount, took a screenshot, and sent it to Press. Maybe facial recognition would turn something up. I also sent it to Snapper so he and Kick could print copies to take to the university tomorrow to show around. Finally, I printed one more copy for Seraphina.

"Hey, Tryst," I said when he answered my call. "Got a minute?"

"For you? Of course."

"There's something I'd like to talk to you about."

"I am at Brix's house. Would you like me to come to your place?"

"I'll come to you."

While the Ridge Estate was adjacent to Los Caballeros, by the time I drove through our vineyards, then theirs, fifteen minutes had passed. When I arrived,

Tryst was sitting out front, on the porch. He stood when I approached, and we embraced.

"It is colder here than at my ranch, but I prefer to be outside, if you don't mind."

"Not at all."

"Catch me up on the search for Luisa Reeve," he said, motioning for me to take a seat.

I told him what we'd learned thus far and what things were still in progress.

"I sense this is not what you wanted to discuss with me."

"It isn't. Although it is related."

He motioned for me to proceed.

"There are two things, actually." I began by filling him in on what I'd read in the report earlier, including the articles about Joseph Reeve's accident and death.

"It was a very sad time with the loss of that family."

"I don't remember hearing about it."

"You were at the university, and I'm sure your parents didn't want to trouble you with news of people you didn't know."

I had been at UC Davis, which was fifteen miles west of Sacramento and four hours from Paso Robles, where my parents spent the majority of their time. I would've been a junior in the viticulture and enology undergrad program.

It was an intense field of study, and given I planned to get a graduate degree as well, I'd had to work hard to maintain my GPA. It made sense my parents wouldn't have mentioned the accident to me, nor my father's purchase of the Reeve property. Ridge acquired new vineyards on a regular basis as they became available.

"I know you said there was more to the story regarding Ridge's purchase of Reeve's vineyards."

"I also said it is a conversation you should have with your father."

I smiled. "I recall. However, is this what you were referencing? Reeve's accident?"

"In part."

I smiled again. "Okay, I hear you loud and clear. Next subject."

Tryst had a glint in his eye similar to the woman's I wanted to talk to him about.

"You know I had a crush on your niece."

Tryst laughed out loud. "A crush, you say?"

"Okay, an infatuation."

He squeezed my shoulder, then his expression turned serious. "An obsession, Noah."

It was rare for Tryst to use my given name, but I understood why he had.

"I feel myself going down the same road with another woman, yet I can't seem to stop myself."

"Seraphina?"

"Yes."

11

Seraphina

My mother was anxious the entire time Press and Beau were in Luisa's room.

"Go see what they're doing," she hissed.

"We know what they're doing. They're looking for anything that might help us find her."

"If there was something in her room, I would have found it."

I was growing weary of my mother's attitude, particularly with her treatment of me. "I'm not the enemy, Mom. I want to find my sister."

"I know you do, baby. I'm sorry I'm so on edge."

"It's understandable. However, I would think you'd be ecstatic to have help, given the police were ambivalent about looking for her."

"I am happy to have help, Seraphina."

"But you don't care for the people providing it—at least one of them."

"There are things you don't understand."

"Are you referring to the wine formulas again? If you are, I'll repeat, you have no way of knowing what happened in the bar that night. You don't know for certain Dad talked to Hewitt Ridge. My God, if he hadn't bought the property, we would have no money whatsoever to live on."

"We didn't anyway."

"Because of the accident."

She lowered her voice. "If Hewitt Ridge hadn't stolen from your father, there would not have been an accident."

I shook my head. "You know, if he were still alive, I could see Dad not wanting to take responsibility for his actions. Knowing four people lost their lives because he drove drunk would be a terrible thing to live with. However, I don't understand why you would blame the Ridge family for something that had nothing to do with them. Formulas or otherwise."

"You weren't there. You didn't know," she snapped.

"Neither were you."

"I mean with your father when he realized he'd have to file for bankruptcy."

I was incredulous. "I was there, Mom."

"You were a child."

"I was eighteen years old. I knew what was going on."

"A child," she repeated.

I stood when Press and Beau came downstairs. "Any luck?"

"We found a shirt in your sister's closet that smells of men's cologne. We'd like to get it tested to see if there are traces of any other DNA. Other than that, not much. How long was she seeing Jorge?" Beau asked.

"Maybe three months."

"Four," said my mother, who stood behind me with her arms folded.

I'd glanced at her over my shoulder but turned my head to look at Beau. "Four," I repeated.

He nodded and turned to Press. "Anything else?" he asked him.

He held up a clear plastic bag that held my sister's shirt. "I'll get this back to you."

I walked them to the door, gave my thanks, and turned around to continue the conversation with my mother, but I didn't see her. I glanced out the window and saw her car pulling out of the building's parking lot. Rather than call to see where she was going, I raced out to my car, intending to follow her. However, when

I got to the main intersection, I couldn't see her car to tell in which direction she'd gone.

"Dammit," I muttered at the same time my cell phone rang with a call from Noah. "Hi," I snapped more than answered.

"Hi. Everything okay?"

"Yeah. My mom is acting strangely again. And before you say it, I know this is hard on her, and I know she's tired, but she's making everything more difficult." I realized the tone of my voice reflected my anger at her, not Noah. "Sorry. Once Press and Beau left, she took off in her car. I tried to follow, but she lost me."

"Any idea where she might have gone?" he asked.

"None whatsoever."

"Would you like help looking for her?"

"I'm not going to look. In fact, I'm thinking about asking her if she wants me to continue staying at the house with her. I get the feeling she might not."

"You're safe. She can lash out at you and you'll still love her."

"She's not a child. As much as she's behaving like one."

"What do you need, Seraphina? What can I help you with?"

Noah's words disarmed me. "A giant hug to start with, then my sister found," I admitted.

"Number one, I can take care of right away. Number two, I'm working on."

"I know you are, and believe me, I'm not complaining. I appreciate everything you and the other guys are doing."

"Where are you now?" he asked.

"Headed to my apartment."

"Want some company?"

"Without it, there's no hug."

"On my way."

I ended the call and looked in the rearview mirror. Two minutes ago, I was furious. Now, I was smiling, thanks to Noah Ridge. The man whose father my mother believed had stolen from our family.

"To hell with it," I said out loud, deciding I couldn't keep playing the things she'd said over in my head.

When I pulled up to my apartment complex, Noah was already there. "Wow, that was quick," I said through my open car window.

"I was already in the neighborhood."

"Ah. Stalking me now, eh?" The look on Noah's face made me wish I hadn't said it. "I'm joking."

"I know." He walked over when I parked and got out. "Come here."

He held his arms out as he approached me, and I fell into them.

"What if she's…"

"Don't go there, Sera. We're going to find her."

"How can you be so certain?" It wasn't the first time I'd asked the question.

"Gut instinct."

He kept his arm around me as we walked to my front door.

"Sorry, I know my place is tiny," I said once we were inside. My furniture even looked too small for him to sit on comfortably.

"We could…Hang on." His phone made a sound like an emergency alert. He took it out of his pocket and swiped the screen. "Be right back," he said, walking out the front door.

I paced in what little room I had to do it in, then decided maybe I should check my phone as well, not that I'd received a similar-sounding alert.

When I didn't see anything, I called my mother, shocked when she answered.

"Mom, I'm sorry. I know this is hard. Beyond hard. I really want us to be able to support each other, not be at odds."

"I know, baby, and I'm the one who's sorry, but I can't explain it better than I already have."

It occurred to me maybe my mother needed a place to direct her anger and Noah's family was the easiest target. "I'm sorry I questioned you about it. You believe what you believe, and while I may disagree, you're right to say I was young when everything happened between you, Dad, and the Ridges."

Noah returned at the same time I said his name.

"Where are you now, Mom?" I asked, mainly so he would know who I was talking to.

"I'm home. I only ran to the store."

"Can I call you back in a minute?"

"Sure, baby, and again, I'm sorry."

I ended the call. "What's happened?" I asked Noah.

"I found a photo earlier today. It was on someone's social media page, and your sister was in it. There was a man in the background, and I asked Press to see if he could get an ID on him."

Someone in the background? "And?"

"Press got a hit. The guy's name is Manual Varilla. He's a Mexican national and on the FBI's wanted list, for outstanding warrants."

I gripped the back of the chair closest to me. "Let me see the photo."

Noah unfolded the paper he held in his hand and gave it to me.

"It's him. *Jorge*. What are the outstanding warrants for?" I felt light-headed, and the room started to spin.

"Come, sit." Noah guided me over to the sofa. "He's believed to be involved in human trafficking."

My sister's "boyfriend" was on the FBI's wanted list for *human trafficking,* and somehow, Noah Ridge believed he and his band of vigilantes were going to find my sister? It was lunacy.

"*Oh my God.* She's *gone.* We'll never find her," I cried as tears streamed down my cheeks. When Noah tried to gather me in his arms, I struggled against him, but he held tight, soothing me.

"We *will* find her, Sera," he said when I went limp, too overcome with anguish to continue fighting.

"*How?*" I stammered.

"Now that we know who he is, we'll use every means possible to find him and bring your sister back home safely."

"It's been *days*. She could be anywhere in the world."

"Press is asking everyone to meet at Seahorse, where we'll start putting together a plan of action."

"Seahorse?"

"His place."

"He calls his house Seahorse?" I didn't really care. I was babbling. Nothing mattered except my sister, who, if she was still alive, was in the hands of the vilest, evilest people in the world.

I got up and raced to the bathroom, where I emptied the contents of my stomach.

"How are you doing?" Noah asked when I returned to the main living area. I couldn't exactly call it my living room since it was also my dining room, office, and bedroom.

"Not great."

"I'd like you to come to the meeting with me."

"Why?"

"One, I don't want you to be alone right now, and two, I want you to be aware of what we plan to do to find her."

"Noah, I'm an attorney, remember?"

"We won't be discussing anything outside the law."

"You're sure about that?"

"Our approach will be the same as a bounty hunter—"

"Except the person who jumps bail signs an agreement when the bond is issued, saying they'll agree to the terms of their release."

"Manual Varilla did exactly that."

"Oh."

"Therefore, we can use all legal means to find and return him to custody."

"Not if he's outside of the United States."

"True. In which case, law enforcement would be engaged."

"Simple as that?"

"Yes, and I'll reiterate. We will not be discussing anything outside the law." He put his hands on my shoulders. "The most important thing is finding Luisa. If you don't want to come to this meeting with me, I'll respect your decision. I'd rather you not be alone, but that's your choice."

"I'd rather not go."

"Understood."

When Noah turned to leave, a feeling of panic came over me.

"Wait."

He led me over to the sofa like he had earlier. "Sera, look at me. Now, breathe with me," he added when my eyes met his. "Slow, steady breaths."

We sat that way for several minutes until I felt my heart rate normalizing.

"Better?" he asked.

"Yes."

"Do you want to reconsider and come with me?"

"Yes," I repeated.

12

Ridge

When I spoke with Press earlier and told him I intended to bring Seraphina with me, it was Zin who'd suggested we meet at Seahorse rather than the Los Caballeros' wine caves, and I agreed. It had to be an alternate location, or I couldn't bring her. I knew as much and never would've considered it otherwise.

"You're sure about this?" Zin'd asked when Press handed him the phone.

"The limitations we face are the same we do with you."

"I don't remember a time when we held a meeting with an outsider present."

"You have a short memory, my friend. I recall it happening less than two weeks ago." Both Addy and her mother had been at Seahorse with the majority of Los Caballeros after she was released on bail. Shortly after our meeting, she and her mother had boarded a private plane—along with Brix, Press, Beau, and Tryst—and were transported out of the country. While Zin hadn't been present when the decision to do so was made, he'd known enough not to be there. The same would be true with Seraphina, except I would be the one ensuring she didn't hear anything that would compromise her status as an officer of the court.

"The DA is like a dog with a bone," he'd also reminded me. "You have to know one of the reasons he hired Seraphina is her connection to the wine industry."

"I know no such thing."

"If you didn't, you do now."

I'd had enough of Zin's warnings about Sera conspiring against Los Caballeros when we were the ones looking for her sister, but there was little I could do to reassure him. Maybe spending time with her today would help.

When we drove through the gates of Seahorse Ranch, Sera gasped. "I'd heard about this place but thought people were exaggerating. This is where you ride horses, isn't it?"

"It is."

"The views are unbelievable."

I had to admit, Press' views were pretty damned good. *Maybe* on par with the ones from my new house on See Canyon Road. Mine, though, were from far above the ocean, whereas Press could walk out his patio door and stick his toes in the water.

"I've heard it was built in the early nineteen hundreds."

"It was, as were several of the outbuildings. However, the main house has obviously been modernized."

I parked the truck, went around to open Sera's door, and walked her over to the main entrance. Unlike my place, which had keypad access, Press' was fancier. I grasped the door handle and waited until a light most wouldn't notice turned from red to green, then went inside.

"Fancy," Sera muttered.

"That's Press."

"Welcome to Seahorse," the man himself said, greeting us. "I know we saw each other earlier, but much has transpired since then. How are you, Seraphina?"

"Fragile," I blurted before she had the chance to respond. "Sorry. I shouldn't speak for you."

"It's okay. It's accurate. I am fragile. As worried as you would expect me to be."

"I believe everyone is here. We can get started."

We followed him into the main room, where the rest of Los Caballeros were assembled. After I made introductions, we were seated.

"Ridge, if you're okay with it, Tryst has a recent update he'd like to address."

It was hard for me to remember I was the senior member of our group when Brix wasn't present. "Of course. Thank you."

"We've called in support from our friends at K19 Security Solutions," Tryst began. "Through their help, we've received intel suggesting Varilla and his crew may be operating out of the port of Yavaros."

My eyes opened wide. "That's less than two hours from your place in Alamos."

"Yes, and I've already engaged people there to begin surveillance in advance of our arrival and K19's. They have been given authorization to immediately act if they see anyone matching Ms. Reeve's description along with any other individuals they deem to be in danger."

"I'll explain who he's talking about when he's finished," I leaned over and whispered to Sera.

"My recommendation is for us to deploy as soon as possible. By us, I mean we divide the team up as Ridge feels is appropriate."

"Agreed," said Press, his eyes meeting mine.

I waited for all those in the room to state their agreement before I voiced my own.

"There is one other matter to be addressed before we leave," said Tryst, who remained standing.

"Please continue," I said.

"Brix and Addison will soon be returning from Big Sur. There are several matters to be wrapped up when they do."

"Is there official news?" I asked.

Tryst turned to Zin. "I believe we'll receive an announcement on two fronts by midweek."

"Should I leave the room?" Seraphina whispered.

"That's excellent news, Zin," I said to him before responding to her. "He won't say more until he's received official confirmation."

"Ridge, Brix asked you to contact him at the end of this meeting," said Tryst.

"Roger that. What is your recommendation as far as when we deploy?"

"We will leave immediately after their return."

"Agreed." I turned to Press. "Would you and Tryst determine who should remain here and who should go to Alamos?"

"We will."

"May I speak?" Seraphina asked.

"Of course," I said.

"First, please know I appreciate your help in finding my sister very much, so when I say this, it is solely out of concern for her."

"Go ahead," I said when she looked at me.

"Can we afford to wait? If Varilla did kidnap her, he may have already taken her out of the country, and if it was to Mexico, she might not be there any longer either."

"May I?" Tryst asked.

"Please," I responded.

"We have reason to believe Varilla is currently in Yavaros. I can assure you, he will not be leaving the port by land, water, or air."

"How—" Sera must've realized mid-sentence she was about to ask a question she wouldn't receive an answer to. "One more thing." She looked around the room as if to warn those present not to challenge her. "I will be on the team going to Alamos."

The only person who commented was Tryst. "As I would expect you to be," he said, looking her in the eye.

When we reassembled at Seahorse for Brix and Addy's return, the mood was far different than when Los Caballeros met to discuss Luisa Reeve.

In addition to the group who had met then, Brix's and Addy's mothers were with us, as was Vader. Alex was too, with her husband and baby girl. Surprisingly, the jab of regret I always felt when I saw her didn't come.

I heard the front door open and turned to see Brix walk in, clasping Addison's hand. I'd never seen my friend looking so happy.

"Addison and I are getting married!" he blurted once they were in the main room, where we were all gathered.

I was first in line to congratulate them, then stepped aside to allow everyone else to do the same. Once they had, I asked for everyone's attention.

"We have another announcement," I said, motioning for everyone to take a seat. Press and Zin remained standing like I was.

Zin cleared his throat. "As we anticipated, all charges have been dropped against Addison." His eyes met Brix's, who stood.

"I have another announcement."

His mother gasped. "Is Addy pregnant already?"

He shook his head and laughed when everyone else did. "No, Mama, but when she is, I'll be sure to let you know so you can be the one to make *that* announcement."

"Go ahead, Brix," I said. "Tell us your news."

"Addison and I have decided to rebuild the diner." He looked between Addy's mother and his. "That's if we can talk the two of you into managing it for us."

Their reaction was the one of joy I'd expected it to be when Brix told me his idea when we last spoke.

Kick and Snapper disappeared into Press' kitchen and returned with a tub filled with bottles of sparkling wine, which they proceeded to open.

"I'm really happy for you," I said, coming to stand next to Brix by the windows that looked out over the Pacific Ocean.

"Thanks. I never dreamed life could be this good."

"I wanted to give you an update on the prosecutor wanting to question Peg and Addy."

"Right. I'd forgotten all about that."

"That's what I was going to say—you can forget about it. She changed her mind."

"I don't care enough to ask why."

"You'll never change, Brix, and that doesn't bother me in the least." I gripped his shoulder. "I'm heading out, but I'll catch up with you later this week."

On my way out, I motioned to Zin, who walked me to the door. "Remember, not a word to him about Luisa Reeve or our impending departure to Alamos."

"Roger that."

"He has enough on his mind right now, and there's no reason for him to get involved in this. Tryst and I discussed it and are in agreement."

"As am I. If you asked, my guess is everyone in this room would also agree—including Brix."

Beau Barrett used the Cessna he and Press owned jointly to travel back and forth from Napa Valley, and regularly utilized their five-hundred-acre mile of shoreline as a landing strip. With the aircraft's maximum travel speed of six hundred miles per hour, we would land in Alamos, Mexico, in a little over ninety minutes.

On board, along with Sera and me, were Tryst, Snapper, and Kick. Press and Beau were piloting and would remain in Alamos with us. Sera's mother was also on board, but so far, she hadn't made eye contact with me. While I didn't understand it, I knew how hard her daughter missing must be and gave her a wide berth.

We'd agreed Zin, Cru, and my brother would remain in Paso Robles unless there was a reason we needed them to join us in Alamos. Conversely, if it appeared Press or Beau weren't essential in Mexico, one or both would return to the States.

While I was busy with Brix and Addy's homecoming, Sera had made arrangements with the DA's office to take a leave of absence. Cooley was well aware of her missing sister, and while he hadn't been of any assistance himself, I doubted he would turn down her request for time off. As far as what else she told him, I hadn't asked and didn't want to know.

I'd told Sera we'd be staying on Tryst's ranch, however there was no real way to describe the place in advance of our arrival. Anything I could say would never do the place justice.

"Welcome to *El Lugar de Curación*, or in English, the Healing Place," Tryst announced when the plane's wheels hit the ranch's airstrip.

In addition to the main residence, there were several guest *casitas* on the property as well as a temple, a building specifically constructed for meditation and yoga, along with outbuildings normally associated with a working ranch.

"You'll be staying in the sunrise *casita* with your mom," I told Sera when a man driving a multirow golf cart pulled up and loaded our luggage onto the back platform.

Press and Beau would be sharing another *casita,* as would Snapper and Kick. Since I was on my own, I'd be staying at the main house with Tryst.

"You said the port where Varilla is rumored to be is only a couple of hours from here?" Sera asked.

"That's right."

"This place is amazing. I can't explain the feeling that washed over me when I exited the plane. It was as though, deep inside, I knew we'd find Luisa."

"I've come here many times when I needed clarity in my life, sometimes not realizing I did until I stepped off the plane."

"My mom seems affected too."

I followed Sera's line of sight and saw her mother standing, eyes closed, facing the sun.

"Are you familiar with the traditional Indian architectural system known as *Vastu shastra*?" I asked.

"I'm not."

"All the buildings on the property were constructed using Vastu principles." I explained it the same way Tryst had to me. Vastu was the science of keeping the five elements of nature—earth, water, fire, air, and space—in balance. When it was applied to building design, the idea was to maximize "positive vibrational energy" in order to create a space that was a spiritual and healing sanctuary.

Sera appeared as skeptical as I had been the first time I visited.

"Later, I'll take you to the temple. It's the most beautiful, magical place here."

"I'd like to see it."

"It looks like your driver is ready." I motioned to the golf cart, where Tryst had led Leah. I walked Sera over to it, and she sat beside her mother. I stood back and waited with Tryst while the others took their seats and the man drove off.

"I don't know how you ever leave this place, Tryst."

"I cannot stay away long."

"I understand why not. I hope I have a similar feeling when my house in See Canyon is finished."

"You can take steps to ensure it."

"Enlighten me."

He chuckled at my pun. "Let's walk and I'll tell you."

Tryst explained it wasn't difficult to apply Vastu ideals to any structure. Given my house was a blank slate other than being built with two stories, it would be easy to make changes to where I intended certain rooms to be.

"Your bedroom should be in the southwest part of the house and on the second story," he said. "Other bedrooms, it is not quite so important."

The rest of what he explained, I'd heard before. For example, the centermost space on the main floor should be empty and, if possible, open through to the second-story ceiling. Certain other things he'd said made sense, such as not putting sleeping quarters or eating areas over a garage or carport.

The only part of the house not complying with Vastu principles were the two west-facing decks. There was a glint in Tryst's eyes when he said he understood why I would be intransigent about eliminating those.

"You *could* add east-facing outdoor spaces too," he suggested, winking when he said it.

When we crested a small hill, I shielded my eyes from the sun and looked out at the main house. It was as though the sun's rays sought it out like a spotlight.

"When will Brix break ground on their place?" I asked, envying the five-thousand-acre wedding gift Tryst had given Addy and him. "Has he said?"

"Work has already begun on the water house and the plans for the main residence."

"He and Addy are going to live here full-time, aren't they?"

Tryst raised a brow. "I cannot imagine Brix giving up the winery entirely. There is also the diner they intend to rebuild."

The Olallieberry Diner had been part of the coastal community of Cambria for many years. When it burned to the ground a few weeks ago, it felt like the heart of the town was missing. I'd been overjoyed to hear Brix and Addy intended to rebuild it and have Addy's mother, who'd owned it when the fire occurred, and Brix's mother, who had worked there in the past, run it. I didn't doubt once it was profitable, Brix and his wife would deed the ownership to the two women.

As far as the winery was concerned, Brix had five younger brothers and one sister, four of whom could take on more responsibility for the family-run operation. Cristobal, the next oldest in the Avila family, was a geneticist whose primary research was conducted at Stanford University.

Alex and her husband owned their own vineyard estate and winery, but I knew Cru, Trevino, Snapper, and Kick would be more anxious than merely willing to take on bigger roles at Los Caballeros Winery.

I would miss seeing Brix most every day, but I understood even if he remained in Paso Robles full-time, he and I would spend less time together now that he was with Addy. I certainly didn't begrudge him that happiness.

"Leah's reaction to you on the plane was perplexing."

I shook my head. "I thought so too."

"Do not take it personally, Ridge. The grudge she holds is not against you."

I studied him. "There you go again, dropping these hints when you have no intention of telling me the full story."

"Have you spoken with your father?"

"He and my mom are in Australia, visiting the Cullens."

Tryst nodded slowly. "It is understandable why you'd wait."

"Noah Cullen is my father's best friend." He was the man I'd been named after. "And you know how close his wife and my mom are. Should I interrupt their time away with something that happened years ago? Was there something wrong with what my father did? From what I can tell, all he was trying to do was help the Reeve family."

He looked off in the distance. "Perhaps."

13

Seraphina

"It's so beautiful here, isn't it?" I said to my mother once we were dropped off at the *casita.*

"We aren't here on vacation, Seraphina. We're here to find your sister."

"I'm so glad you reminded me. It had slipped my mind." I walked outside, letting the door close behind me. Evidently, I was wrong about the attitude adjustment I'd thought I witnessed in my mother when she got off the plane. She was back to acting as though I couldn't possibly understand how she felt.

I saw a building in the distance I guessed was the temple and took off on foot in that direction. Once I was close, I noticed Noah walking toward it from the opposite way.

"I was coming to see if you wanted to visit the temple with me," said Noah.

"I needed to take a walk. My mom and I aren't getting along very well."

"I could say the same about Tryst."

My eyes opened wide.

"Nothing to do with you or Luisa."

"Something with my mom?"

He studied me. "I'm not sure."

"What the hell happened back then, Noah? From what I remember, your father did our family a huge favor when he purchased the vineyards and winery."

"I wish I knew."

"But you think there's more to the story too?"

He shrugged. "Tryst seems to want me to think so, not that he'll elaborate."

"What did he say?"

"He keeps saying I should talk to my father about it. However, my parents are in Australia. When I told Tryst my plan was to wait until they returned to the States to ask my dad what had happened, he gave me the impression I shouldn't."

"Wait?"

"That's right. However, it's not something I feel comfortable discussing over the phone. The last thing I want to do is blindside my dad while he's out of the country on holiday with my mother."

"Hmm."

He smiled. "Exactly what I thought."

"I understand why you'd want to wait."

"You do?"

I nodded. Now didn't feel like the right time to tell Noah what my mother had said about his father stealing my dad's formulas. Especially since I couldn't prove it and neither could she.

Even if she could, I didn't believe the formula they'd used to produce the Vineyard Twenty-Seven Blend was anything my father had developed. If he had, he would've needed to file a patent to record what the exact varietals and percentages of those varietals used were. If what Ridge Winery produced varied in any way from the exact formula, there'd be no patent infringement. Either way, to my knowledge, there weren't any patents filed in the first place.

"What's on your mind, Seraphina?"

"There are three sides to every story. The first party's, the second party's, and somewhere in the middle is the truth."

"I completely agree."

We'd reached the temple and walked up the large steps made of concrete. The structure itself was built of brick with the exception of the wooden door and the steeple, which also appeared to be made of concrete but with several openings in it that looked like windows.

Once inside, I understood why. The only light came from those windows and small lamps made to look like candlelight. The ceiling where the windows were was conical-shaped and lined with sandalwood. There was also a similarly shaped altar made of the same wood lining the inside of the steeple.

"It's so beautiful," I said, taking it all in. I pointed to a pew. "Can we sit?"

"Absolutely," Noah said, motioning me into the row. "It's magical, right?"

"Oh yes. It's like what I felt when I got off the plane intensified."

"I feel the same way every time I come here."

"When we find Luisa, I want to bring her here. To heal."

Noah leaned back and put his arm around me. "That's the reason Tryst said he wanted you to come to the ranch. Your mother too. So when we do find her, you can all heal."

I felt my eyes fill with tears and tried to blink them away.

"Can I ask you something, Sera?"

"Of course."

"How did you convince your mother to come to the ranch?"

It hadn't been easy, and eventually, I'd guilted her into it by reminding her if I was in Mexico, I might not be able to communicate what was happening with the search for Luisa.

"My mother wants to find my sister as much or more than I do. Setting aside differences of opinion is easier to do at a time like this."

"Interesting way of putting it—differences of opinion."

"I'm not sure what else to call it."

He nodded. "It's a mystery to me."

"Me too."

Noah said he and the others would soon leave for Yavaros. While he wasn't sure when he would return, if there was anything to report, he'd be in touch. Tryst, he said, would be staying here with us, in the event we needed anything. He also shared the contact information for each of the guys who'd traveled here with us.

When I returned to the *casita*, my mother was napping. I walked into the main room and noticed one wall was lined with shelves of books.

When nothing caught my eye to read, I dug out my laptop and did a search for Los Caballeros.

The majority of what I found led me to a Mexican criminal organization known as Los Caballeros Templarios—or the Knights Templar Cartel—based in the Mexican State of Michoacán. Between feuds with rival gangs and a mass arrest of their leader and several of his associates, the reign of the cartel had lasted fewer than seven years during the twenty-tens decade.

Historically, the first mention of a similarly named organization dated back to the fourteen hundreds.

Then, the Knights Templar defeated the Moors and took control of a town, Jerez, in southwestern Spain. They renamed it Jerez de los Caballeros—direct translation: Jerez of the Knights. Whether the secret society stemmed from there or not was part of the mystery.

Other than Los Caballeros Ranch—a dude ranch in Arizona—and the winery belonging to Brix's family, the search yielded no further results.

When DA Cooley assigned me to the "task force" to take them down, I'd requested previous case files. I was told to do my job and gather my own evidence. In other words, there weren't case files because there was no proof.

The question I should've asked Noah the morning we'd met for breakfast when I threatened Brix and Los Caballeros, was why William Cooley had it in for them. It made no sense to me. I couldn't say for certain the county sheriff was in cahoots with them, but based on his interaction with Brix, Noah, and Tryst the night of the Wicked Winemakers' Ball, he was definitely friendly with the men accused of heading it up.

Now, though, I had direct information indicating a "group of vigilantes" did exist. Within that group, there was an obvious hierarchy, witnessed when all those present at Seahorse Ranch appeared to defer to Noah. The question was, had they broken any laws? Certainly not to my knowledge. And as Noah had said, their search for Varilla was no different than that of a bounty hunter or even that of a private investigator.

Every rumor I'd heard about them indicated their alleged actions were for the greater good, not anything nefarious.

It was almost as though they formed a collective superhero. I laughed at the thought, but if I had to liken them to any one "thing," that would be it. They were like Superman or Batman, coming to the rescue when they were needed. They took no credit, no payment, wanted no accolades.

So, again, the only thing that made sense was Cooley harbored some kind of grudge against Los Caballeros or Brix Avila.

"What are you doing?" my mom asked, coming into the room where I sat.

"Work."

"I thought you took a leave of absence."

"I did. I still have some case reports to finish up."

"Are you hungry?"

I was, now that she mentioned it. "Would you like me to make you something to eat?" Not that I'd looked to see if there was any food in the kitchen.

"I can do it."

I set my laptop on the coffee table and joined her, stunned to see the refrigerator and pantry were both loaded with fresh fruit, vegetables, tortillas, what looked like already grilled chicken and carne asada, as well as several other ingredients.

My mother and I took a plate of tacos out to the porch along with a pitcher of lemonade and two glasses.

"Mom, I want to ask you something about Dad."

"Go ahead."

"Do you know if he filed any patents on his wine blends?"

"I'm certain he did not."

Which meant, on the outside chance she was right about Hewitt Ridge stealing my father's formulas, there was no legal means to pursue such a claim.

"Did Dad tell you Hewitt stole them?"

She shook her head. "He didn't need to."

"What does that mean?"

"I figured it out on my own."

I decided to be as relentless as she was. "How?"

"I did. That's all you need to know."

"No, Mom, answer the question. *How* did you figure it out?"

When she stood to leave, I got up too. "You can run away, but you won't get far, Mom."

"You're not funny, Seraphina."

"I'm not trying to be. Noah Ridge has done nothing but try to help us. You should be thanking him rather than shooting him nasty looks."

"I don't shoot nasty looks."

"No? The next time you do it, I'll take a photo so you can see for yourself."

"He's not innocent, Seraphina."

I wanted to pull my hair out. "What does that *mean*?"

"The Ridges act like white knights, coming in to save the day, but they're not. They're the villains."

"Have you spun this into a fairy tale where Dad, who drove drunk and killed an entire family, is the hero? And Hewitt Ridge—along with his son, apparently—are the evil landowners who forced him to do it? I call bullshit, Mom. Even if Hewitt was at the bar the night of the accident, he didn't pour the liquor down my father's throat."

"I can't do this." She turned to go inside, but I grabbed her wrist.

"You hurl accusations without anything to back them up. You vilify two men who have been kind and decent to us, but when it comes down to explaining why, you speak in platitudes, expecting me to go along with you based solely on your word. You weren't there that night, Mom. You don't know what happened. You don't have proof Hewitt stole anything." I shook my head. "I can't do this, either." I stormed off the porch, leaving my mother and my dinner behind.

The sun was setting, but there was enough light from the moon so I could see where I was going. Rather than walk in the direction of the temple, I went toward the building Noah had pointed out as the meditation room. I could certainly use several minutes of quiet reflection, during which I hoped I could clear my mind of my mother's antics.

I was about to open the door when Tryst walked out.

"Hello, Seraphina," he said, putting his hands together and giving me a slight bow.

"Hello, Tryst. Thank you for bringing us to your ranch. As Noah says, it is a magical place."

"Join me for a moment?" He motioned for me to sit on a bench in front of the building.

"Sure."

"I came here when I was a young man serving in the military. Truth be told, I was lost. Or I was guided here intentionally by a higher power. I knew, one day, I would save enough money to buy a small plot of land and build a home."

"Instead, you built a ranch."

He smiled. "I did. My wife and I spent many happy years here."

"Do you have children?"

"No. Rosa and I could not conceive."

"I'm sorry."

"Fortunately for me, my brother and his wife had no problems doing so. I have six nephews and one niece, who I am as close to as if they were my own children."

"They're lucky to have you in their lives."

"Mutually lucky." He looked out at the horizon. "I named this place *El Lugar de Curación*, the Healing Place, hoping a miracle would happen while we were here and my Rosa would be healed. It did not."

"I'm sorry," I repeated.

"I tell you this so you understand that no matter how much we want to heal those we love, it is not always within our power to do so."

I wasn't sure whether Tryst was speaking in generalities or meant someone specific in my life. Either way, the first person who came to my mind was my father.

There were days I wished I could go back in time and figure out a way to save him from himself. However, Tryst's words reminded me that even if I had tried, it might not have been in my power to do it. He would've had to want it for himself. "I think somewhere in the back of my mind, I know what you're saying"

"Your mother is in a great deal of pain, but she must be the one to do the work to make it go away."

At first, I was too stunned to speak. Then I remembered Noah saying he was troubled by things Tryst had said to him. "You aren't going to elaborate, are you?"

"It is not my story to tell. My sole purpose in speaking with you about your mother is to offer my support should you need it."

"The two of you should be the ones having this conversation. You're equally cryptic."

"I know it's difficult, but try not to take your mother's troubles personally. They have nothing to do with you. I said the same to Noah."

"About my mother?"

"Yes."

"I'm going to ask you one question, and I would appreciate it very much if you would answer."

He nodded.

"Did my mother have an affair with Noah's father?"

14

Ridge

I would be the first to admit I was way out of my element once we arrived at the docks in Yavaros. If I had been here before, I didn't recognize it now. It was nothing like the small port I'd expected it to be.

There were rows and rows of warehouses, shipping containers stacked twenty deep, and ships lined up for what looked like miles, waiting to be loaded before setting off to places around the world.

That Tryst could've assured Seraphina Varilla would not be leaving the port city by land, air, or sea seemed impossible to me, given the sheer amount of opportunities he would have to do so—particularly by sea. Judging by the look on Press' face, he agreed.

"Are you certain this is where we're intended to meet?" he asked his brother when we arrived at the specified location after the sun had set.

Beau looked at something on his phone, then around where we stood between two rows of the stacked containers. "Yes, this is where Ares said to wait."

"Ares?" I asked.

"Son of Zeus and Hera. God of war. The more violent aspects of it anyway," Press responded.

I rolled my eyes. "Thanks for the lesson in Greek mythology, Master Barrett. Who is this guy connected to?"

"K19, but their Shadow Ops team," Beau responded.

When we were at Seahorse, Tryst had mentioned calling in support from K19 Security Solutions. The private security and intelligence firm was founded by Kade Butler, oldest son of Laird and Sorcha, whose vineyard estate and winery were on the other side of Los Caballeros from ours. Kade, who had served in the military special forces, followed by a stint with the CIA, was Alex Avila's husband's older brother.

The Central Coast wine region's community was small and tight-knit—which proved to be both good and bad.

A man who I immediately knew was Ares came around the corner. He might as well have been the model the Marvel character of the same name was fashioned after. Which was the reason I'd recognized the name and knew he was an Olympian God—not that I'd admit it to Press.

I was a big guy, but Ares was taller and had more muscle mass.

"You must be Ridge," he said.

"I am," I responded, trying not to cringe when he shook my hand.

"This is Press and Beau Barrett."

While the former shook Ares' hand, Beau waved from more than an arm's distance away.

"Your job tonight is to stay out of the way and as invisible as possible until we need you," Ares said, looking at each one of us and handing us a comms device.

We had been briefed before arriving that our purpose for being at the shipyard tonight was twofold. One, to identify Luisa Reeve if the Shadow Ops team found where human trafficking victims were being held. Two, to help transport the victims to a place where they could receive necessary medical care as well as to begin the reunification process.

Tryst had stayed behind in order to line up the medical personnel, who would remain on standby. He'd also asked the people who worked for him on the ranch to be on standby as well for any help that might be needed.

"How many men do you have going in?" I asked.

"Six, and from what we can tell, there may be as many as thirteen people being held in that container over there." He pointed three stacks down and one row over. "As far as what we're up against, based on thermal imaging, there's a total of sixteen inside. We believe the other two people who appear to be moving about are with Varilla."

"Are you sure it's him?"

"Since it's on the word of two different informants, we're as certain as we can be. Can you positively ID him?"

I shook my head. "I've seen one photo, and it wasn't a close-up shot."

Ares looked at Press and Beau, who also shook their heads.

"Fortunately, we had more than that to go on."

"There's someone at Alamos who could," I muttered.

Ares nodded. "We'll keep that in mind if necessary. Our intention is to keep the three assailants alive enough for questioning."

Alive enough. It wasn't the first time I'd heard it phrased in such a way.

"One more thing. Are you all armed?"

"Affirmative," I responded before Beau could, knowing he'd be more likely to say something closer to "locked and loaded."

We were able to keep track of what was happening through the comms, so we knew the precise moment the team of six made their move into the shipping container. First, we heard shouting, followed by gunshots and the sound of people screaming.

The next thing we heard sent a chill down my spine.

"Let her go, Varilla. The container is surrounded. There's no way out," Ares shouted.

"You let me go, or she dies," said a man who sounded as much like he was from California as I did.

"If she dies, you die."

"Traer el coche," I could hear Varilla say through someone's comms who must've been standing close to him. The other thing we now knew was he had comms of his own and had used them to summon transport.

Within seconds, an SUV with blacked-out windows barreled up to the back of the shipping container, tires screeching. Press, Beau, and I had our weapons out, ready to fire if given the command to do so.

"Four incoming," I said as they jumped out of the vehicle.

"Take 'em out!" Ares responded.

I fired first, followed a split second later by Press, then Beau.

"Three down."

The SUV was parked close enough to a security light that I could see the fourth man duck behind it.

"I've got him," said Beau, creeping around at the same time Press and I fired several shots to distract the guy. A few seconds later, I heard one more and saw the man fall to the ground.

Through the comms, I heard one more shot go off right after Beau's had, then several more.

"Goddammit! *You stupid motherfucker!*" Ares shouted. *"Hold your fire!"*

"She's dead," said another voice.

"He's not."

After making sure the four men who'd arrived in the SUV were all dead, I asked permission for us to come inside.

"Proceed in," said Ares. I could barely hear him over the sound of sirens blaring as they got closer.

My legs felt like fifty-pound weights were on each ankle as I walked through the back door of the container, not wanting to see the woman who'd lost her life, but knowing I had to.

"Please, God, don't let it be Luisa," I whispered.

15

Seraphina

If Tryst told me I needed to ask my mother if she and Hewitt had an affair, I swore I'd haul off and belt him. Fortunately, he didn't.

"I do not think so," he said instead. "However, I do believe she met with Hewitt without your father's knowledge."

"What about?"

"I'm uncertain."

"If you had to guess," I snapped. None of this was Tryst's fault or doing, but I'd had enough of this shit.

"Then, I would say it would have been to ask for help."

"Was this before or after the accident?"

"Before. Maybe after as well."

"How do you know this?"

"I saw them."

"Before?"

Tryst nodded. "Yes."

"Where?"

"Outside the Ridge winery building. Your mother appeared to be crying."

I drew in a deep breath. "Did he comfort her? Embrace her?"

"Not that I saw."

"Where were you?"

"The Avila estate borders Ridge's."

"Were you close enough to hear what either of them said?"

He shook his head.

Was this how she knew Hewitt had stolen the wine formulas? Had my father gone to the bar that night to confront him based on something my mother told him? If that was the case, I wondered how she could've held in the guilt all these years.

"She said Hewitt stole something from my father."

"I cannot say one way or another whether that is true."

"Have you heard rumors to that effect?" I felt like I was leading an interrogation.

"I have not."

"I'm sorry, Tryst."

"There's nothing for you to apologize for. You're seeking answers. Unfortunately, I do not have them."

"Can I be honest with you about something?"

"Always." He reached over and patted my hand.

"I don't want to talk about any of this until we find my sister."

"I will be honest as well."

"Go ahead," I said when he hesitated.

"You and Noah will need to resolve these things between your families before you're able to move forward with your future."

"Tryst...I...I don't know what to say."

"Let me walk you back to the *casita*," he said, standing and holding his hand out to me. I took it and stood to follow him.

It wasn't a long walk, but it was a quiet one. When we reached the porch, Tryst put his hand on my shoulder. "It's as important for you to be honest with yourself as it is with other people."

I watched him walk away until the moon went behind a cloud and I could no longer see him.

Before I went inside, I made a decision. I'd tell my mother we would not be discussing anything to do with Ridge Winery or Hewitt Ridge until after we found my sister.

When I opened the door, I saw a single light on, in the kitchen. The plate of tacos sat on the table, covered with plastic wrap.

It was better that my mother had gone to bed. I felt drained after my conversation with Tryst, and I was also worried we hadn't heard anything from Noah.

I grabbed a blanket and went out to the porch. I pulled the chair farther out so I could see the moon and sat down. The clouds were no longer covering it, and I could see more stars.

After my father's accident, we endured four long years of him remaining in a coma. As it was explained to us at the time, he was in a deep state of unconsciousness. There were indicators of brain stem responses and spontaneous breathing.

Given my father was not "brain dead," my mother would not consider removing him from the fluids and nutrition keeping him alive.

"The doctor said your father could recover consciousness," she'd repeat even though my sister and I'd stopped asking.

I remember the phone ringing late one night, a rarity in our house, and my mother's wail of anguish. I also remember feeling sad, but for me, my father had died four years prior. I'd never believed he would recover.

It was far harder on my sister. Luisa was twelve when the accident happened and sixteen when my father passed away. There were so many things she didn't understand, and kids at school were merciless to the point I suggested my mother homeschool Luisa.

She would come home in tears after being taunted as a murderer's kid. "They say I should've died instead," she'd tell me. Since I was over eighteen, I was the one who'd contacted the school and pleaded with them to intervene with the bullying, but I never got anywhere. The only reason the principal had considered talking to me was because everyone knew my mother spent her days at the hospital, with our comatose father.

Luisa graduated and was accepted into Cal Poly, but she'd remained wary of making friends. She did, but it took a long time to gain her trust.

I could see someone like Jorge recognizing her insecurities and preying on them. She was especially vulnerable, having lost her father at such a young age. And really, she'd lost her mother too.

Luisa was the reason I'd never considered getting a job very far from home. I thought about suggesting we both relocate once she graduated.

I closed my eyes, raised my face to the moonlight. "Please, God, keep Luisa safe. And Noah too."

16

Ridge

"It isn't her," I said out loud even though no one had asked me to determine if the woman Varilla had shot and killed was Luisa Reeve. Perhaps they already knew it wasn't, but I hadn't.

None of the other women being held in the shipping container were her either. It wasn't only women, though. There were men too. As Ares had said, there were thirteen in total. The youngest looked to be a teenager.

They were huddled together with nothing more than the clothes on their backs. No blankets, no cots, no sign of food or water. Depending on the intended destination, a ship could take a month or longer to get from one port to another.

Also, based on how few people there were versus how many the container would hold, I couldn't help but wonder if there were more victims being transported here from another location. Maybe food and water were due to arrive with them.

I watched as Ares and one of the other K19 guys moved Varilla out. He wasn't dead, thank God. He deserved to be, but first we needed answers.

Press, Beau, and I began helping the victims out of the container and into a warehouse where a triage center was being set up.

"Bones, what are you doing here?" I heard Beau ask as I was on my way back to the container to help move more of the victims.

"Dalton?" I said, feeling profound relief at seeing my brother. We walked toward each other and embraced. "Tryst said my help was needed down here and arranged for a private plane to bring me to the ranch."

"Whose?" asked Beau.

My brother shrugged. "K-something."

"K19," I said rather than asked.

"I heard there's a triage set up in one of the warehouses. How bad is it?" he asked.

"It could've been much worse had the container actually been loaded onto a ship. As it is, many of the victims are dehydrated. Some show signs of being beaten," Beau told him.

"I'd better get over there."

"Thanks, Dalt."

He cringed as he walked in the opposite direction. "Can't you call me Bones like everyone else? Dalt has always sounded like dolt."

He'd managed to get back at me by calling me No, saying it would be too weird to call me by *his* last name like everyone else did.

"What's happening with Varilla?" I asked Press.

"You don't want to know."

"Has anyone gotten anything out of him about Luisa Reeve?"

"Nothing specific."

"Fuck."

"However, Ares said he has reason to believe she's alive."

I supposed that was good news. "But where?"

"He's working on that bit of information now." Press looked around as if to see if anyone was within earshot. "Varilla wants to make a deal," he said in a lowered voice.

"For what?"

"Luisa's whereabouts. In exchange, he walks."

"How about, in exchange, he doesn't die after being repeatedly tortured?"

"I'm certain Ares said something along those lines. The problem is determining whether Varilla actually knows or he's bluffing."

"Of course."

"Have you contacted Seraphina?"

"Not yet. I'd rather do it in person and after I have something more definitive to tell her." It was also going on three in the morning. "What about Tryst?"

"If you're asking if he's told her anything, the answer is he has not. He's waiting for word from you on whether you want him to," said Press.

"I do not."

"I'll pass that on. By the way, was that your brother I saw going into the triage center?"

"It was. Evidently, Tryst arranged for someone from K19 to transport him here."

"Listen, Ridge, why don't you return to Alamos? It may be hours, or longer, before Ares is able to get anything out of Varilla."

Given we'd driven down in two separate SUVs, there was no reason I couldn't leave on my own. Alamos was close enough for me to return, in the event I was needed. "Roger that."

By the time I arrived at Tryst's ranch, it would be closer to five, and I'd go straight to Sera's *casita* and give her an update—such as it was.

The drive was almost as arduous as the long walk into the shipping container when I was faced with the possibility the woman Varilla had killed was Seraphina's sister. While the news I had to tell her wasn't as heartbreaking, that we hadn't found Luisa was.

I'd hoped against hope I'd receive word from Press, saying Ares had managed to get Varilla to give up Luisa's whereabouts before I reached Tryst's ranch, but the call hadn't come.

The only thing Press did report was he was able to learn from the port's cargo operations that the specific container we'd been in was scheduled to be loaded on a ship the following day, heading to the Yangshan Port in Shanghai, China. It was the world's biggest and busiest container port.

I was stunned to see Sera sitting in a chair on the porch when I drove up. She was covered with a blanket.

I parked, got out, and walked over to her. "Hey," I said when she opened her eyes and looked up at me.

She sat up straighter. "Hey."

"Did you sleep out here?"

"I guess I did."

I reached under her, gathered her in my arms, and carried her inside. She rested her head against me. Rather than setting her on her feet, I brought her into the bedroom with the open door and gently set her body on the mattress. When I sat beside her, she snuggled against me. We sat in silence, holding each other, both innately knowing what we needed now more than anything was comfort. Eventually, she looked up at me.

"We didn't find Luisa."

Sera put her head down and tightened her arm around my midsection.

"We did find Varilla, along with people being held in a shipping container bound for China."

"You found Varilla?"

"According to the man interrogating him, he wants to make a deal in exchange for revealing Luisa's whereabouts. Ares, the guy questioning Varilla, believes she's alive."

"What does Varilla want?"

"To be let go."

Sera shook her head.

"While that won't be happening, I'm sure they'll meet somewhere between Varilla's freedom and death."

"What about the other victims?"

"They're being given medical attention at the same time the team is arranging reunification with their families." I left out the part about the one who was deceased, along with the deaths of Varilla's accomplices.

"You said the container was bound for China?"

"Yes, to Shanghai." I closed my eyes, loving how Sera felt in my arms, wishing there was a far different reason her body rested against mine.

"They could have been sent anywhere once they reached the mainland."

I held her closer to me, wishing I had different news.

"Noah?"

"Yeah?"

"Thank you for being honest with me. I know it isn't easy to be when there's so little information."

I leaned down and kissed her forehead. "You're welcome."

"Is it okay if I don't want to get up yet?"

I smiled. "More than okay. I'll go—"

"I don't want you to get up, either." She shifted to her side, and I did the same. Her back was to my front, and that is the way we both fell asleep.

When I woke, having no idea how long we'd slept, the bedroom door I'd left open was closed, which meant her mother had to have seen us. While I didn't care if she had, I'd told myself I'd give Leah a wide berth out of respect. Falling asleep with her daughter in my arms wasn't something I would've done intentionally.

Sera rolled her body toward me, nuzzled against my neck, and murmured something unintelligible. I closed my eyes and drifted into a deep sleep.

When I woke a second time, I was alone, stunned I hadn't roused when Sera got out of bed. I could hear voices coming from the kitchen. Relief washed over me when they didn't sound argumentative.

I checked my phone for messages, but when I didn't see any, I wondered if Press and Beau had returned to the ranch yet. After stopping by the bathroom, I went into the kitchen, where Sera and her mother were still talking.

"Good morning," I muttered, running my hand through my hair and wishing I'd tied it back rather than leaving it hanging loose.

"Good morning, again," said Sera. Her mother nodded in my direction.

"I should head to the main house. My brother is here, by the way."

"Your brother?"

"Dalton is a doctor. Tryst arranged for him to fly down last night to help." I wasn't sure how much Sera had told her mother, so I didn't elaborate.

"I'll walk you out," she offered. "Thanks for staying with me," she said once we were outside.

"How's your mom?"

"Okay. Wondering what the next step is, the same as I am, but accepting we may not know yet."

"I'll see what I can find out. Press and Beau stayed on in Yavaros when I left, but I haven't heard from either one of them since shortly before I got here last night."

Sera wrapped her arms around me and rested her head against my chest. "You don't mind me doing this, do you?"

I put my arms around her too. "Not at all." In fact, I wouldn't mind more of it. However, now wasn't the time for me to pursue a romantic relationship with Seraphina Reeve. First, we had to find her sister. Then we had to figure out what had transpired between our families. Once those two things happened, I had every intention of letting Sera know how much I wanted to spend more time with her. As much time as she'd let me.

When I leaned down, intending to kiss her forehead, her lips met mine. It felt like the most natural thing in the world. It was chaste and quick, but perfect.

"Sorry," she said, her cheeks flushing.

I put my hand on her chin and tilted her face so I could see into her eyes. Then I kissed her again. "I'm not sorry," I said before stepping back and walking to the SUV. I didn't look until I got in but was relieved to see Sera standing in the same place she had been, her fingertips on her lips.

When I arrived at the main house, Press was behind the wheel of an SUV about to park. My brother and Beau were inside. I got out and walked over to it when Press lowered the window.

"Nothing to report from Varilla yet. Ares is still working on him."

Dalton got out and walked over to me. I put my arm around his shoulders. "How'd it go in triage?"

"The worst of what we saw was dehydration. As Beau said, some signs of physical abuse. Any longer in captivity, and I'm sure their conditions would have gotten much worse."

"What about reunification?"

"K19 is handling most of it. Their resources are unbelievable," said Press.

He was the techno-gadget geek among us, so his words didn't surprise me.

"Listen, I need to get some sleep, and I'm sure Press and Beau do too," said my brother.

"Ares knows to include you in any communication," said Press.

"Roger that."

"How's Seraphina?"

"Hanging in there. Seemed to take the update in stride. For now, at least. I'm sure she's as anxious as we are for Ares to get something out of Varilla."

Press nodded.

"Do you happen to know if anyone from K19 asked cargo operations if the shipping container bound for China had another destination scheduled?" I asked.

"I'm glad you brought it up," said Beau. "No. In fact, Yangshan was confirmed as its 'final destination.'"

Which meant someone intended to get the human trafficking victims out of the container while it was still at the port. From there, God knew where they'd be transported. After thanking Press and Beau, I followed Dalton inside.

"You've returned," Tryst said to me. "Welcome to the ranch, Bones," he said to my brother.

"It's been too long since I visited."

"Agreed. I'm sure you're both exhausted. Bones, you can take the second bedroom on the right." Tryst pointed to the hallway. "I expected you earlier," he said to me once Dalton left the room.

"I went straight over to talk to Seraphina when I arrived this morning." He didn't ask for further details, and I didn't offer them. At least about falling asleep with her in my arms. "Have you been thoroughly briefed on what went down last night?"

"I spoke with Press by phone earlier."

"So you know the container was destined for China."

Tryst nodded.

"I think I'll return to Yavaros later and see if I can locate information about other containers going to the same destination in the last week."

"I believe Snapper and Kick are looking into it now."

"The container wasn't full."

Tryst had been looking at his phone but raised his head.

"It could easily have held twice the number of people, and there was no food or water."

"You believe Luisa Reeve, along with other victims, may be somewhere here, in Mexico."

"Maybe. It doesn't make sense she wouldn't be with Varilla, though."

"Unless something happened to her."

I thought the same thing but hadn't intended to say it. "Or she was in another container, headed to a different destination."

17

Seraphina

"Not a word, Mom," I said, walking into the house after Noah drove off.

Her eyebrow was raised, but she remained silent. I went into the bedroom, pulled clean clothes out of my suitcase, and walked into the bathroom to take a shower.

As much as I didn't want any shit from my mother about Noah, I refused to beat myself up about him, either. He was a good man, and I was attracted to him. On top of both those things, I found it so easy to be with him. Maybe it was that my brain had no room to second-guess him or myself with all the worry I felt over my sister. Either way, I had no intention of questioning it.

When he held me as I slept, I felt safer than I had since Luisa went missing. It wasn't that I believed myself to be in danger; it was more my fear for my sister and what might happen if I let go of the tight grip I had on my emotions.

While I showered, I thought a lot about Noah saying Varilla wanted to make a deal to disclose Luisa's whereabouts. As an assistant district attorney, I made deals every day of the week. The hardest part was explaining them to the victim's family. I'd always believed myself to be empathetic to their plight.

Now, though, I was trying to put myself in the interrogator's shoes instead. He or she walked a fine line between letting someone who belonged in prison off on too little punishment and, in this case, making a deal to find one of his victims.

As much as I wanted to beg Noah to give him whatever he wanted if he'd tell us Luisa's whereabouts, I knew it was impossible. Before any deals could be struck, the negotiator had to verify whether Varilla actually had the information he was offering. If it were me handling a case like this one, nothing would be on the table until there was proof of life. I had no doubt the person doing the negotiation would demand it, at the very minimum.

In order to get through each day, I had to believe my sister was still alive. I refused to give up hope. However, I couldn't sit idly, doing nothing. I needed somewhere to focus my attention. Since I couldn't come up with anything useful to help find Luisa on my own, I planned to research the Vineyard Twenty-Seven Blend, hoping to disprove my mother's theory that Hewitt Ridge had stolen my father's formulas. According to my mother, no patents had been filed. Later, I'd do a search to confirm none were held in my father's name, which would mean she'd have no way to pursue the man criminally. Any lawsuit would be in civil court. In which case, the burden would be on the defendant to prove innocence.

Not that she'd suggested pursuing the matter. She probably reasoned the same way I had that a winery the size of Ridge would be diligent about filing all necessary legal documentation, including patents.

"Would you like to take a walk?" I asked her after I'd finished in the bathroom.

"Where?" Her question threw me. All she needed to do was look out the window to see the options were limitless.

"There's a meditation room I thought about visiting this morning." I'd intended to last night but was waylaid by my conversation with Tryst.

"I'm fine here."

"We could explore other parts of the ranch. The temple is really lovely, Mom."

"I'll stay here, baby."

I nodded and gave her a hug. While I knew I had to do something or my anxiety would skyrocket, maybe for my mom, staying alone at the *casita* would be her own form of meditation.

It had been a long time since I attended a yoga class, but I remembered enough to be able to do a simple workout. I was finishing when I heard the door open.

"Sorry," said a man I didn't recognize when I looked over my shoulder to see who had come in.

"It's okay. I'm done." I got up and wiped my face and neck with the towel I was glad I'd remembered to bring.

"I'm Seraphina."

"Dalton Ridge," he said, shaking my outstretched hand.

"I see the family resemblance."

"My brother takes that as a compliment."

I chuckled. "Noah said you're a doctor."

"I am." He walked to the back of the room and opened the door of a cabinet I hadn't noticed. Inside were yoga mats and towels.

When he didn't say anything else, I walked toward the door. "Have a good workout."

"Hey, we'll find your sister."

"Thanks." I went outside and sat on the same bench I had last night. Rather than feeling energized, I felt deflated. I appreciated Dalton's comment, yet it left me feeling cold. There were no clouds today, but the sun did little to warm me.

"Good morning, again."

I opened my eyes and looked into Noah's. "Hi."

He sat on the bench, beside me.

"Are you joining your brother for yoga?" I asked. "If you are, don't let me keep you."

"I didn't realize Dalt was here, but no, I was looking for you."

"Any particular reason?"

Noah put his arm around me, and I rested my head on his shoulder. "Lots of reasons, but the main one is I missed you."

I closed my eyes when tears threatened. I felt the same way. The chill I'd experienced had nothing to do with Dalton's arrival or his words, but rather with my disappointment over him walking in rather than his brother.

"I missed you too." I sighed, knowing I had to ask. "Have you heard anything about my sister?"

"Nothing definitive. Varilla is still refusing to talk without a deal."

"We need confirmation she's alive first."

I felt him nod. "I also heard from Snapper about another shipping container owned by the same holding company as the one we found last night, except rather than leaving for China, it's headed for the Port of Felixstowe, in the UK."

I raised my head. "From Yavaros?"

"No. From the Port of Altamira on Mexico's eastern coast. The team we're working with is tracking the ship's route and current location now."

I sat up straight. "When did it leave?"

"Two days after your mother said your sister went missing."

"What is the transit time between the two ports?"

"Eight to ten days."

I stood. "We need to find out if Luisa is on that ship. She disappeared seven days ago, which means it could arrive in as few as three days."

Noah pulled out his phone and swiped the screen. "Now we're getting somewhere."

"What's happened?"

"Varilla has bigger fish he's willing to give up. However, no protection will be offered without confirmation Luisa is alive."

I sat down, closed my eyes, and prayed. When I opened them, Noah was still looking at his phone.

"Is there more?"

"It appears there is." He positioned his phone so I could see a message was being typed. We both watched until the marching dots went away. "Guess not."

"I'd like to go to the temple."

"Would you like me to go with you?"

"Please."

Noah stood and held his hand out to me. He didn't let go until we were walking up the steps. Then only to open the door.

"I can come in or wait out here."

I looked up at him. "How about this? I'd like you to be with me whenever you can, unless I say otherwise."

"That's true for me too."

The same serene feeling came over me as soon as we walked through the door. While my fear for Luisa lingered, it wasn't predominant. Rather than sitting in a pew, I approached the altar, knelt, raised my face, and prayed. Noah was beside me, close enough for our arms to touch.

I'd silently said amen and opened my eyes when Noah pulled his phone out.

"She's on it."

I didn't need him to say who or on what. My sister was on her way to England, and when the ship transporting her there arrived, I would be there.

"When can we leave?" I asked.

"Arrangements are being made now. My guess is, within a few hours."

"I need to tell my mom."

I rushed out of the temple and ran toward the *casita*.

"Mom!" I called out, racing from room to room once I arrived. "Mom? Where are you?"

"She must've gone for a walk," said Noah, who had been looking into rooms like I had. "I'll ask Tryst where she is."

I walked outside while Noah talked to him.

"Please let Luisa be okay," I said, looking up at the sky. I hated that it was the best I could hope for, but after what she'd been through, how could it be more?

"She's at the meditation building," said Noah, joining me on the porch.

Her being there seemed odd, but maybe she was looking for me.

It was a short walk, and when Noah opened the door, I saw her inside, talking to his brother. Tryst arrived at the same time we did.

"Mom, we have news. We know where Luisa is." I realized my blunder as soon as I finished my sentence. I should've said we *believed* we knew.

"Why are you here? Why aren't you—"

I interrupted my mother. "Jorge confirmed she is on a container ship bound for England."

She studied me.

"We're assembling a team to meet the ship when it arrives at the port," Noah explained.

My mom looked from him to me.

"I'll be going with them," I told her.

"What should I do?" she asked.

"It would be best if you stayed here at the ranch," said Tryst before I had the chance to respond.

I looked at Noah, and he nodded.

I reached over and squeezed her hand. "I'll be in contact and keep you informed every step of the way."

18

Ridge

I was glad Tryst had suggested Seraphina's mother stay here in Mexico. If it had been me, I couldn't help but wonder whether she would've agreed so easily. As it was, I wasn't sure Sera should be there when the raid took place. Because that was the plan—a full-blown raid.

While Varilla claimed Luisa was on the container ship bound for the UK, the parameters for his deal remained the same. Until we had confirmation Luisa was alive, nothing was officially on the table. Him telling us she was on the container ship was merely a concession.

A text from Ares said a more detailed brief was sent via a secure server. I excused myself from the group gathered and went outside. If necessary, I'd return to Tryst's place and read it on my laptop.

When I logged on, the first piece of information I saw was we'd be on a flight scheduled out of the Ciudad Obregón Airport at fifteen hundred.

Second, as opposed to only one container transporting victims, Ares reported intel suggested there could be as many as ten. After seeing the one in Yavaros, my guess was one the same size would hold twenty, maybe thirty people. While the victims could be drugged, it would still take two or three men to guard them.

Thus, a full-scale raid was being coordinated between K19 Shadow Ops, US Immigration and Customs Enforcement, the UK's National Crime Agency, and Military Intelligence Section 5—Britain's equivalent of the US Department of Homeland Security. Ares also mentioned Interpol was on standby, should further assistance be required.

K19 was sending at least four from their Shadow Ops team and had requested support from the six of us from Los Caballeros who'd participated in the raid on the single container in Yavaros. Our main role would be victim assistance.

Given the container ship's arrival time likely couldn't be pinpointed until the day of, K19 and Los Caballeros would remain on standby two hours away, in London.

I sent a message, requesting Seraphina Reeve be permitted to travel with us, but I didn't get an immediate response. Worst-case scenario, I would fly with her commercially and make arrangements for her to stay at the same hotel in London.

"I see you read the brief," said Press, joining me outside the meditation building.

"Ten containers? *Jesus*."

"On this ship alone. According to Ares, it's the reason the bigger guns are coming from his team's parent organization."

"This is the first I've heard."

Press nodded. "Ares only mentioned Doc Butler by name, but evidently, there are more traveling with us."

I didn't know Kade, aka Doc, well, although we'd met a handful of times at winery-related events.

My phone vibrated, and I saw a response from Ares, saying there was no problem with Sera traveling with us.

"Everything okay?" Press asked.

"Until Luisa is found, nothing can truly be okay, but for now, at least we have an idea of where she might be and a plan of action."

"I concur. Also, K19's involvement is a godsend. Without them, I doubt we could've managed the rescue on our own."

I completely agreed.

While Press had offered their plane for the trip to the UK, particularly since it was already in Mexico, Ares declined, saying K19 had one en route.

When we boarded, several other people were already on the aircraft. The only one I recognized was Doc, who greeted and introduced us to the rest of the group.

"These are my partners Razor Sharp and Gunner Godet. We have Mantis and Alegria Cassman in the cockpit, and this is my wife, Merrigan." He motioned to the woman exiting the restroom. "Farther back are Dutch and Malin Miller."

After I'd introduced each of us, I pointed out the Shadow Ops team members also on the plane to Seraphina. I only knew them by their code names. "That's, uh, Cayman, Kodiak, and Puck," I said, not exactly sure who was who.

Doc's wife approached. "Seraphina, I'm glad you're traveling with us. I want you to know the team is committed to keeping your sister safe."

"I appreciate you saying so."

"I asked Malin to participate in this op because of her experience in the Middle East. She knows much about the plight of exploited women and will be a good source of support. Alegria is a pilot but will be assisting with the victims once the rescue portion of the mission is complete. Do you have any questions?"

"Can I help?"

"Certainly. However, let's put your participation on standby until we know how your sister is doing. She's your first priority."

"I agree."

"As you have probably guessed, I'm from the UK and have requested assistance from previous co-workers along with translators and medical personnel. The more female support we can put in place, the more help we'll be to the women."

"How will you get them back to the US or wherever they were taken from?" Sera asked.

"We'll arrange for private transportation."

"Not by ship."

"No, not by ship. By plane."

I reached over and squeezed Sera's hand.

"Any other questions at this time?" Merrigan asked.

"I don't think so."

Doc's wife smiled. "We have a long flight, so if something else occurs to you, don't hesitate to let me know."

Sera said she would and thanked Merrigan, who took a seat closer to the front of the plane, next to Doc.

"How are you doing?" I asked. She'd been quiet since we found her mother at the meditation building.

"Out of sorts. Overwhelmed. Worried. More than worried—frantic."

Everything she was feeling was understandable. I'd give anything to take away all the negativity Seraphina was experiencing, but until we found Luisa, nothing could.

"I was about to say my life is in limbo, but it makes me sound like the most awful person. My sister is in a shipping container, experiencing God knows what kind of horrors. I have no right to complain about anything."

"You're human, Sera." I put the armrest between us up and wrapped my arm around her shoulders.

"When we get to the hotel, I've arranged for you to have a room of your own," I said after explaining those on board would remain in London until we received official word when the container ship would arrive at Port Felixstowe.

"Where will you be?"

"I'm sharing a room with Dalton."

Sera looked out the window, but turned back when I put my hand on hers.

"Hey, remember earlier, when you said you'd like me to be with you whenever I can?"

"Unless I say otherwise."

"At times, I'll also need you to say it *is* what you want."

"Like now?"

I smiled. "Exactly."

"If you wouldn't mind and if it's possible, I'd like you with me until we find Luisa."

"I can do that."

"Ridge…"

I waited a few seconds to see if she'd continue. "I know, Sera." For now, our relationship and what may come of it was also in limbo, but I was in no hurry. As she'd said, God knew what horrors her sister might be experiencing.

"You do? Okay."

When I heard Mantis announce from the cockpit that we'd be landing soon, I woke, surprised both Sera and I had slept through most of the flight. Since we had a few more minutes, I waited to wake her up, knowing how much she needed the rest.

I guessed we'd be in London for at least two days, maybe longer. In that time, I didn't doubt K19 would be doing the necessary prep work in advance of the raid.

I wasn't sure how much those of us from Los Caballeros would be asked to participate. Probably very little. Which meant we would have a lot of time on our hands, making the hours spent waiting for word feel endless.

"Do you have family still living in England?" I leaned over and asked Press.

"My grandparents have a place near Eaton Square and another in Southwold. They're likely in the latter presently. Why?"

"Time will drag, sitting in a hotel all day."

Press hit his forehead with his hand. "Why didn't I think of that? There'll be plenty of room at their place for the lot of us to stay."

"I don't know which hotel we're booked in, but it can't be far from Eaton Square."

"I believe it's under a mile." Press looked behind him. "I'll talk it over with Ares."

When I nodded, he stood and walked toward the plane's aft, where the man sat.

"What's going on?" Sera opened her eyes and raised her seat from the lying to sitting position.

"We'll be landing soon."

She checked her watch. "I can't believe how long I slept."

"You needed the rest."

"He doesn't see it as a problem," said Press, retaking his seat.

"What, or shouldn't I ask?"

"Our group will be staying elsewhere," Press said to Sera.

"Elsewhere?"

"Press has family who own a place in London. He believes they're away presently."

"It's actually three places. Triplex apartments in the same building. It's where we lived and is quite nice. The best part is there's a common area for the family to gather, but they have totally separate quarters when we prefer not to."

"You're sure they won't mind?" I asked.

Press raised a brow. "I'm the oldest grandson. I wouldn't go so far as using the term prodigal—that would be my brother. However, they'll be delighted to have us use the place." He shook his head. "Apologies. Poor word choice. not that I can think of any better."

It was midday London time when we deboarded the plane. Ares said transportation had been arranged to take us all to the hotel, so it wasn't a problem to drop us off first. He also said we'd reconvene for a briefing at zero nine hundred the following day.

Press' grandparents' building—which was a more appropriate term to use than "three apartments"—was as swanky as I would've expected it to be, knowing his parents and him.

The apartments were all about the same size by square footage. However, one had four bedrooms, another had three, and the third had two. Press said he and Beau would stay in the one with the fewest.

"I'll be staying with Seraphina for the time being," I said after motioning Press away from the others.

"Understood. The two of you can stay in the one on the far right, and we'll put the boys in the middle. It has four bedrooms."

I had no idea what to anticipate after the raid and rescue operation, but if we needed to remain in England for any length of time, it might work out to stay here then as well since there'd be room for Luisa.

"I know I slept the entire flight, but I'm still so tired," Sera said after Beau showed us to our quarters.

"I recommend following what your body is telling you it needs."

"Noah?"

I'd been looking out the window, but turned when she said my name.

"I don't know what to expect."

I walked over and sat beside her on the sofa. "I don't either."

"It may sound as terrible as my complaining about my life being in limbo, but I don't want to learn more about human trafficking. What I'm imagining my sister is going through is horrific enough. I don't need confirmation that it's actually worse."

What I'd discovered about traffickers was worse than I imagined, so I understood her trepidation. "I know this sounds impossible, but try your hardest not to think about it. I know it may seem trite—"

"It does."

"I'm sorry, Sera—"

"Don't be," she said, interrupting me a second time. "I understand, and it's what I've been trying to do. You're also right to say it sounds impossible, because it is."

"What has helped you until now?"

"Convincing myself she's 'somewhere' and fine and, when I do find her, she'll tell me how sorry she is for worrying me when she was sunning herself on a tropical island."

"Where would she go? Is there a place the two of you traveled to together?"

"We went to Greece when I passed the bar. We had almost no money, so it was bare bones, but we still had the time of our lives."

"Tell me about that trip while I get us something to drink."

"Do you think, uh, never mind."

I raised a brow.

"Wine, and I'm sure they have a selection to choose from."

I wasn't certain there would be any in this apartment, but I had no doubt Press would be able to tell me where to get my hands on a couple of bottles. I'd made arrangements for one very special bottle of wine to be sent to the hotel, which I'd pick up in the morning. However, that one, I'd save for Sera, Luisa, and I to share. Or for the two of them to have on their own. When I went into the kitchen, though, I found a fully stocked wine cooler. "Red or white?" I asked.

"If there's both, white, please."

I located two glasses, nicer than the ones I owned, and that was saying something since they were a gift from my mother. I uncorked an exceptional white wine from the Friuli region of Italy, poured two glasses, took them into the living room, and handed one to Sera.

"Be right back." I'd also found an assortment of crackers along with a selection of cheeses I put on a plate and set on the coffee table.

"Now, tell me about Greece."

19

Seraphina

An hour ago, I wouldn't have believed anything would make me feel better, let alone smile or laugh, but here I was, doing both.

"Thank you, Noah," I said, holding up my glass to toast.

"I loved hearing about your adventures and have to admit I've never been a fan of Ouzo, so your warning about what happens when two people drink an entire bottle between them only reinforces my dislike of it."

"You dislike Ouzo? How is that possible?"

"Licorice. Never been a fan. In fact, the smell turns my stomach."

"But…"

He cocked his head. "What?"

"The Vineyard Twenty-Seven Blend."

"What about it?"

"I've always found it to have noticeable notes of black licorice."

"I try not to focus on it. There's plenty of stone fruit to balance it."

I laughed. "You really dislike it that much?"

Noah nodded. "If you were eating it right now, I'd have to leave the room."

"Speaking of eating." I pointed to the nearly empty plate. After two glasses of wine, I was hungry, and not for more cheese and crackers.

"How hungry are you?" Noah asked, looking at something on his phone.

"Famished."

"There's a place a couple of doors down that Press highly recommends. He said it requires a 'relatively adventurous palate.'" The last part, he spoke with an English accent, mimicking his friend. "He said it's nearly impossible to get a reservation except if you're a Barrett, evidently. If we'd like to try it, he'll call and see what he can do."

I shrugged. "Might as well try it. Although with your issues with something as mundane as licorice, are you sure you qualify as adventurous?"

His left brow went up. "How about a wager? The person willing to try the least number of dishes pays the tab."

"It doesn't count if I can't eat more because I'm full."

Noah shook his head. "It's a tasting menu. Whoever *tastes* the least, pays."

"You're on. Wait. Does it have a decent wine list?"

He tapped his phone's screen with his finger. "One of the best I've ever seen."

I could blame the two glasses of wine I'd had on an empty stomach for not realizing Noah was looking at the menu when he made the wager. However, I was determined to at least taste everything we were served.

Our first course consisted of turnips and crab with house-made bread and chicken butter. I was onboard with everything but the poultry-inspired spread. However, I did taste a tiny bit, and it was heavenly enough to eat a healthy serving more.

The second course was a tame-sounding ricotta, peach, and bean dish. The creamy cheese mixed with the beans was good, but the peach gazpacho served with it was fantastic. Knowing another six courses were coming, I refrained from eating every morsel of it.

Scallops with cucumbers and almond were followed by a potato, truffle, and artichoke dish. Both were fabulous.

My biggest challenge was the langoustine with pork fat and burnt apple, but like everything else, the pork fat, which I was sure would turn my stomach, was yummy.

I was feeling overly full when sea bass with aubergine and tomato was served followed by lamb and mint, which were accompanied by a zucchini-seaweed salad.

"I surrender," I said when the final course, a dessert made of strawberries, sheep's yogurt, and pink peppercorns, was put in front of me. "Please bring the tab to me," I said to the waiter.

"I'm sorry?" he said with scrunched eyes.

"The bill? Check?" I looked from the confused man to Noah, realizing he'd already taken care of it.

"That's hardly fair. I lost the wager," I said when the waiter walked away.

He shrugged. "You made a valiant effort. Besides, you did say it wouldn't count if you couldn't eat more because you were full."

"Yes, but you tasted everything too. We should've at least split it."

I did manage a small taste of dessert before Noah requested it be boxed to go.

"See? You won, after all. I didn't try this one."

"You let me win."

He shrugged. "I like seeing you smile, Sera."

I realized I had been for most of the evening. While part of me felt guilty for enjoying myself when my sister was in the bowels of hell, I knew Noah's only agenda was to help keep my mind off the next few days.

I didn't doubt they'd be the hardest of my life. Harder than seeing my father languishing comatose for four years.

"Thank you," I said as we walked two doors down to the apartment. "Both for dinner, and for keeping my mind off my sister for at least a little while."

"You're welcome."

I tucked my arm through his and was about to rest my head on his shoulder when Noah abruptly spun around.

"Stay behind me."

With my face buried in his back, I watched him pull out his gun, then put it back.

"Come on, let's get inside."

"What happened?" I asked once we were safely in the apartment.

"I overreacted."

"To what?"

"I saw someone watching us. When he reached in his pocket, I assumed it was for a gun."

"What was it?"

"A phone."

"That's odd. Someone menacing-looking enough you believed they'd pull a gun?"

"I believe he may have been taking photos."

"Of us?"

20

Ridge

"We'll be following a different protocol for the remainder of our time here," I said while, at the same time, messaging the guys in the other apartments, asking if they were available to get together briefly. Within a few minutes, we'd assembled in the common area as Press suggested.

"When we left the restaurant tonight, I caught someone photographing Seraphina and me."

"It could simply be because you're staying here," said Press.

Beau nodded. "It happens."

"I'd still prefer we take every precaution when leaving and returning to the building. Is there another exit?"

"There are three other ways to go in and out."

"We'll use them randomly. Also, I don't want Sera here by herself. I'll remain at the apartment during tomorrow's briefing."

"I'll stay," said Dalton. "It would make more sense."

I agreed and said so after Sera nodded in agreement too.

"We'll take a walk later and see if anyone is staking out the place," offered Snapper, pointing to Kick and himself.

"I'll check the apartment's security footage as well," said Press.

Once everyone left, I walked over to Seraphina and put my hands on her shoulders. "Are you ready to call it a night?"

"I am."

"Would you like—"

"Yes," she answered before I could finish my sentence.

I smiled. "Go ahead, then."

"Go ahead with what?"

"Whatever it is you thought I was going to ask."

"What *were* you going to ask?"

"If you wanted to shower before going to bed."

"I would."

"Go ahead, then," I said, motioning toward the bathroom.

"Wait. Don't you want to know what I was saying yes to?"

"A bedtime story?"

Sera smiled. "Something like that. Would you mind, I mean, would it be too weird if we…"

"Shared a bed?"

"Yes. That. Too weird?"

I moved my hands to her waist. "We both know there's a strong attraction between us. We also know the timing isn't right for us to explore that attraction. So, no. It isn't too weird. It's about helping you get through the next few hours, the next few days, in one of the only ways I can. I will hold you while you fall asleep, Sera. And if you decide you want me to, I'll tell you a bedtime story."

After we'd both showered and got into bed, Sera fell to sleep within minutes of her head hitting the pillow. It took me slightly longer, only because I kept waking myself to make sure she was still asleep. Finally, I couldn't fight it any longer.

There were many reasons I preferred staying here over the hotel where the K19 team was ensconced. The level of privacy and security this place afforded was definitely one of them. The other was its close proximity to the meeting site.

The next morning, the five of us each left the building through different exits and at intervals.

"Anything look out of the ordinary?" I asked Press when he arrived in the lobby a few minutes after I had.

"Not presently. However, I did spot someone watching the place last night when I looked at the security footage. As I said, it could very well be paparazzi. Regardless, we'll proceed with caution."

"I didn't realize you and Beau were the sort to attract the tabloids."

"We aren't. However, we have a cousin who is."

"Does he stay at your grandparents' place often?"

"I can't say whether it's often. I do know he visits from time to time. By the way, Snapper and Kick checked the footage when they returned and said they saw the same guy."

Once the rest of our crew arrived, we took the elevator to the eighteenth floor, where we'd be meeting in one of the suites.

"Good morning, gentlemen," said Doc, opening the door when we arrived.

It wasn't long before Ares asked us to take a seat so we could get started. "Who's missing?" he asked.

"My brother stayed behind with Seraphina. We were followed by a photographer last night—"

"Take this offline," he snapped, motioning for who I thought was Cayman and me to step out of the room.

"Sorry. He's a little tightly wound this morning. He gets annoyed when someone usurps his briefings with something not on the agenda," said the man with the British accent. Given he was the only one of the four Shadow Ops here who spoke with one, I was relieved when I guessed his name right. "Anyway, tell me about this photographer."

I explained how I'd noticed someone taking our photo on our way to the apartment after dinner and how Snapper and Kick had gone out to take a look. "They saw the same guy Press did on the security footage."

"Have that forwarded to us immediately."

"Press already—"

I stopped talking when he sighed.

"Roger that," I muttered instead of telling him Press had already run the image through facial recognition and nothing had turned up. The other thing I didn't bother to tell him was how both Press and Beau believed the man was with the paparazzi, or that *he* appeared as tightly wound as Ares did.

Given our conversation took all of two minutes, Ares was still in the preliminary phase of briefing the plan once the container ship arrived in port.

Based on the information he'd received from the cargo operations center in Altamira, he'd created three-dimensional images of the containers and pinpointed the locations where those belonging to the same holding company that had booked the one out of Yavaros would be. The images appeared on a large-screen monitor.

"As you can see, there are eight highlighted. Some are in the interior as well as at the bottom of their respective stacks. There are two more the guy at cargo operations said were booked under a different name but he believed might be affiliated. Those are indicated here and here."

Unlike the others, those two were mid-stack. I looked at Press, who raised his head.

"Yeah?"

"They're at the bottom of the stacks."

"That's what I said."

"Then, they can't be soft tops."

"Correct."

"They're transporting people. How in the bloody hell do they expect them to live?"

"It's a damn good question. Given the cost to ship all these containers, they had to have devised a method to get air inside these things, or you're right. They'd be transporting corpses."

"Jesus," I said under my breath.

"Right there with ya," said Doc. "I've seen too many horrific things in my life, and this is near the top."

I couldn't imagine what he'd *seen* that would be worse, but I didn't want to know and hoped he didn't elaborate.

"Kodiak will take over from here and outline our plan of attack."

The graphics changed from the ship to the yard. "Plan A is to have the containers moved to a single location, ready for transit. Or that's how it will seem. Instead, we'll be isolating them." Another three-dimensional image appeared, indicating how and where they'd be off-loaded.

"Where it becomes problematic is how long it will take for all the containers to be moved off the ship, since they're in different locations and, for the most part, on the bottom, so the last to be off-loaded. It could be several hours."

"How is that problematic?" asked Snapper.

"Since we don't know who or what is inside, at least until we're able to make use of thermal imaging, we run the risk of whoever is in the first container, alerting whoever is in the others."

"Worst-case scenario?" asked Ares.

Kodiak shook his head. "A bloodbath."

"Won't that happen anyway if the raid takes place at the docks? The way they're being off-loaded will be a dead giveaway." Snapper winced. "Sorry. Bad word choice."

"Which leads us to Plan B."

The second option Kodiak outlined was to wait until the containers were picked up for transport to their next destination. According to the manifests obtained from

Altamira, each of the ten containers was slated to go to a different location. Raids would take place en route.

"There's still the problem of whatever guards are inside, communicating the raid to the others," said Gunner, who was standing off to the side with Doc's other partner, Razor. "Same bloodbath. No offense, gentlemen, but your plan is way too complicated."

"What's plan C?" Doc asked him.

"I don't give a fuck who tells who what. The first thing we do is scramble all communication. We board the goddamn ship the minute it arrives in port—en masse—and we open every one of the containers on your drawing," said Gunner.

Kodiak shook his head. "It isn't that simple. Logistically, it's impossible."

"No, it isn't. We get to those containers the same way deck hands would if one caught fire or was leaking or if they believed there were stowaways in it—*or fucking victims of human trafficking*. Is it hard? Damn straight, it is, but we're talking about over two hundred lives. *Innocent lives.* I'm not standing around with my thumb in my ass, waiting."

"He's right," said Razor. "Thermal imaging will give us a road map to priority containers."

I had to agree. It seemed like the solution with the best possible outcome.

The idea of waiting would be painfully hard, especially for Seraphina, and for me, having to explain it to her. Her patience already exceeded what mine would've been. If my brother was believed to be locked in a container where he may or may not be able to breathe, I didn't know how I'd stop myself from intercepting the ship while still out on open waters.

Doc stood. "Regardless of the plan we implement, there are inherent risks to the victims. Our goal is to get them to safety and do everything we possibly can to keep them alive while we're at it. The loss of one life in Yavaros was a painful reminder that we do what we can, to the best of our ability."

After those in the room nodded or spoke their agreement, Doc turned to Gunner. "My vote is you proceed with your plan." Then he turned to Merrigan.

"I'm in complete agreement. My intention is to focus solely on what happens once the victims are rescued." She looked over at me. "We'll work on that now, yes?"

"Yes, ma'am," I responded.

"Ares and Kodiak, let's powwow with Razor and nail this shit down," said Gunner.

There were many things I admired and appreciated about the K19 team assembled in this room. One was how they knew better than to make every mission decision collectively. Too many cooks in the kitchen, as they say.

I couldn't imagine the logistics of Gunner's proposal, but I didn't need to. It wasn't my lane. With the number of agencies involved, I had no doubt the full-scale effort to be mounted would be successful.

While US immigration had been mentioned, I assumed the UK's Custom and Border Protection would have to be involved as well. The ship would no longer be in open waters; thus, the port authority would be required to abide by UK law. When I asked Merrigan about it, she confirmed they would be.

"If there's nothing else you need from me now, I'll switch places with my brother and return to the apartment," I offered.

"Actually, why don't we head there together? I'm sure Seraphina could use a distraction. We'll have her be part of the planning process for the work to be done after the rescue has taken place."

She and I were on our way out when Ares announced the container ship was due in port in approximately thirty-six hours. That it would arrive after nightfall would work to our advantage.

"Snapper and Kick, Razor requested the two of you stick around," Ares added. While a small part of me wondered why, a much larger one only cared about returning to the apartment and seeing Seraphina.

21

Seraphina

"You really don't have to stay in the apartment with me," I told Dalton after what felt like an endless amount of time feeling as though I had to make polite conversation when what I really wanted to do was ask if he'd heard from his brother.

"Noah and the other guys should be back soon," he responded, checking something on his phone. "Wait. Correction. Noah and Merrigan are on their way."

I got up and walked over to the window, wishing I had some way to work through my anxiety. Waiting was hell. Not as bad as what my sister was going through, though.

I saw a car pull up in front of the building. Noah got out first, followed by Merrigan. I moved away from the window and sat on the sofa. Dalton stood when they walked in.

"How are you holding up?" Merrigan asked, walking straight over to me and sitting down.

"Trying to remember that no matter how hard this feels, what my sister is experiencing is much harder."

"It's difficult when we feel powerless. Especially when we're the kind of woman who usually is not."

I nodded, wondering why she was here. Surely, it wasn't only to console me.

"I'll let the three of you talk," offered Noah, who had walked to my other side, leaned down, and kissed my forehead. It was such a familiar gesture, and while I suppose it should've made me uncomfortable, it felt reassuring.

"Stay, please," said Merrigan. "In fact, let's move to the table, yes?"

She pulled a laptop out of her bag.

"Should I get mine?" I asked even though I had no idea why we'd moved to the table or what we were doing.

"Yes. We all should."

Dalton excused himself to his apartment, saying he'd only be a minute.

"I asked Ridge if we could work on the action plan for when the victims have been rescued from the containers."

"Containers? How many are there?"

"We believe there are eight. Perhaps ten."

I felt sick to my stomach. This wasn't a matter of twenty or thirty people being trafficked. This could be two or three hundred.

"We'll need to set up a triage center on the same scale as we would a catastrophe with a large number of victims," she said once Dalton returned. "I don't have much experience with this sort of thing, but we'll have support from people who do."

"I do," said Noah's brother. "We'll start with a basic intake station, then prioritize by condition." He turned to me. "Please understand that we need to be prepared for all possible outcomes."

"I do."

Noah was seated beside me and squeezed my hand.

"We'll separate victims into four categories. 'Minor,' or those needing little to no medical attention. The second category will be what we refer to as 'Delayed.' For those victims, they may need an IV for hydration, but otherwise, we'd anticipate their condition to be stable."

He was creating an outline on his screen and turned his laptop so we could see it.

"Next would be 'Immediate.' The victim will need immediate medical attention—classified within twenty minutes or less. Finally, while we don't anticipate having victims in what is medically referred to as 'Expectant—'"

"Pregnant?" Noah asked.

Dalton shook his head. "In this instance, it refers to those unlikely to survive. The focus, then, would be on palliative care and pain relief."

He turned the screen toward him. "In Yavaros, we were able to make use of an empty warehouse. In looking at photos of the shipyard, quite a few structures would fit the bill. The unknown is whether any are empty."

"I'll find out," Merrigan offered.

"Let me," said Noah. "I'm the least help here."

He stood, walked a short distance away, and placed a call.

"We should start mobilizing supplies as well as medical personnel. Do we have an ETA on the ship?" Dalton asked.

"Yes. It's expected in approximately thirty-six hours," Merrigan responded.

Noah was still on the phone but approached the table. "Press said he and Beau can go to Felixstowe now. According to the terminal, there are several empty warehouses."

"Clear it with Ares first," she said without looking up from something she was typing on her computer.

"Roger that," said Noah, walking away again.

"I'm working on mobilization," Merrigan said to Dalton. "How soon do you want personnel to begin arriving?"

"Given when the ship is scheduled to arrive, I'd like to get the triage center set up as soon as possible. Support personnel can arrive in as few as three or four hours prior."

"The containers won't be off-loaded immediately," said Noah.

"Right."

"I'd like to head there now myself," said Dalton. "What did Ares say?"

"Cayman is the point man at the port. He's traveling there with Press and Beau. From what Press said, MI5 has been alerted, as was customs and border protection."

Merrigan looked up again. "All teams are beginning mobilization, including victim response and support." She turned to me. "I understand you will want to be there for your sister."

"Yes."

"You must prepare yourself."

I nodded. "I can do this."

She looked up at Noah but didn't say anything. I saw him nod.

"Very well. We should prepare to leave as well. Anticipate it could be two or three days before we return to London. Perhaps longer. While it's only two hours one way, it's the round trip that becomes problematic."

"Copy that," said Dalton, standing and closing his computer. "I'll continue working on the basic plan on our way there."

"Kade will be here in thirty minutes and will bring what I'll need. Can we all be ready to leave by then?"

"I'll be ready before that," I told her.

"As will I," added Noah.

"Very well. I'll tell my husband to step on it. I'll also tell him to bring food. It's hard to say when we'll get the chance to eat again."

I left the room to put away what little I'd unpacked last night while Noah did the same.

"I can sit in the back," I offered when we were getting in the SUV.

"You and Noah take the second row. I'm going to be working on the triage plan the entire way."

Since no one spoke for the first several minutes after I'd eaten one of the sandwiches Kade brought, I felt myself getting drowsy.

"Put your head on my shoulder and sleep," said Noah, putting his arm around me.

"It feels like it's all I've been doing."

"Stress takes a heavy toll on your body. Besides, like eating, who knows when we'll get the chance to sleep again."

"He's right," said Merrigan, looking over the seat. "Sleep while you can. I plan to do the same."

22

Ridge

Upon our arrival at the port, it didn't appear much was happening outside what would normally take place at a terminal as busy as Port Felixstowe. However, behind the scenes of the mission, as Ares referred to it, there was a flurry of choreographed activity.

While the members of Los Caballeros may have seen ourselves as would-be secret agents, what I witnessed proved what we did was so far beneath what occurred in real life. I was almost embarrassed.

"We help in whatever way we can," said Press when I shared my perception. "Without us, Addison Reagan would still be sitting in a jail cell, waiting to go on trial for murder."

He made a good point, but I wished he hadn't said it in front of Seraphina. It wasn't that I didn't trust her; it just seemed a little too "in her face." Especially when she appeared to wince.

"Sorry," I said to her.

"There's nothing for you to be sorry for, and what Press said is true. We in the justice system don't always get it right. And when we do, it isn't always timely. On the other hand, while Los Caballeros may consider themselves good guys, not every band of vigilantes is. Enforcers in organized crime, for example. To them, they may be protecting their own, but at what cost to everyday citizens, who look to law enforcement to keep them safe?"

Was it my imagination, or was the tone of her voice the same it had been the morning we'd met for the breakfast we never ordered? I tried to focus on the "good guy" comment rather than the organized crime enforcers protecting their own. As hard as I tried not to bristle, I couldn't help it. Based on Press' expression, he had the same reaction.

"Ridge, a word?" he asked.

Seraphina stalked off in Merrigan's direction without saying anything else.

"What in the bloody hell was that about?" he asked when we were far enough away that she couldn't hear us.

"I was hoping I was overreacting."

"We 'may consider ourselves good guys'?"

"Try to be cognizant of her frame of mind presently."

"Did you or did you not say you were hoping you were overreacting?"

"Compared to you…"

"Sod off. You better hope she isn't compiling evidence to use against us. I'd hate to be the generation responsible for the demise of an organization that's been in existence for four hundred years."

"Again, as long as we're not overreacting."

Beau approached at the same time I finished my sentence. "What are the two of you talking about? You look like you're about to come to blows."

"Nothing like that. We're all a little tightly wound right now," I said before I walked away, repeating what Cayman had said about Ares earlier.

There was no way in hell Seraphina was doing what Press was suggesting after we'd helped save her sister's life. *No way.* Deep inside, though, maybe I was also questioning whether she would.

Since the warehouse where the triage area was set up also served as the command center, it was where the majority of meetings took place between the entities carrying out the mission as well as terminal, cargo, and berth operations.

Gunner, Razor, and Kodiak, along with the team from customs, were meeting with the terminal operations manager. When I walked away from Press, they motioned for me to join them.

The current discussion was in regard to the order the containers believed to be holding human trafficking victims would be opened. What I'd envisioned as a one-by-one process was, in actuality, a plan to access as many as five at a time.

"Why not all of them?" asked Gunner, pointing to a schematic of how the ship was loaded. "This ship isn't full. Not even close."

The terminal guy shook his head. "Logistically, it isn't feasible."

"Let me ask you this. If these containers were leaking dangerous or flammable chemicals, how many could you get to at once?"

The man sat back in his chair and rubbed his balding head with one hand. "We'll see what we can do."

Gunner leaned forward and leveled a steely glare at the man. "Tell ya what. If there is a single loss of life, I'll see what I can do to not hold you responsible."

"This is why I love you, Gunner," said Razor when the terminal guy got up and walked away. "Don't like the answer someone gives you? Make it so they give you one you like better."

"Two hundred lives, Raze. At least." When the man shifted in his chair and turned his head away, I could swear I saw him tear up.

While, earlier, I'd thought about how different we were from the people who worked for K19, the amount of care we had for the victims didn't vary at all. This was as personal to Gunner as it was to me. Maybe not to Seraphina, but damn close.

"Can I ask how this will work?"

Razor and Gunner turned to Kodiak, who pointed to the schematic. "As you heard Gunner say, this particular ship isn't full, which makes what we're asking the longshoreman to do more feasible." Access to most of the containers was easy since they were on the lowest level of the stacks. For the two that weren't, he explained an elevation platform would allow access to those thermal imaging indicated were holding the victims as opposed to cargo. The platforms were large enough to accommodate as many as ten people.

"The thermal imaging will give us an idea of how many are in each container. To a certain extent, we can determine movement," Razor added.

"We'll use standard SWAT procedure for entering. Distraction tactics, shit like that," muttered Gunner. "Our primary goal is to rescue the victims and keep them alive."

"Before we attempt entry, the entire ship will go dark," Razor explained. "And by distraction tactics, what Gunner means is noise—"

"Loud fucking noise," said Gunner.

Razor glared at him. "The idea is those inside will have no clue what's happening on the outside."

"It won't mask the sound of the container doors opening since those *sonuvabitches* are heavier than shit, but at least we'll have some element of surprise on our side."

"What if the ship arrives before nightfall?" I asked.

"Easy. We wait. It isn't like the traffickers are gonna open the door to see what's goin' on," said Gunner.

I didn't ask what would happen after the container door was opened. As Gunner said, the primary goal was to rescue the victims and keep them alive.

Ares received regular reports on the ship's predicted arrival time from the terminal operations manager, and according to his last update, the ship was scheduled to arrive thirty-one hours from now, so on target for the middle of the night.

I scanned the room in search of Seraphina and saw her talking with Merrigan and my brother. On my way to join them, Press intercepted me.

"There's something you need to see."

I followed him in the opposite direction of where I'd been headed. He sat at a table with his back to the wall and opened his laptop.

"What is this?" I asked when he turned it so I could see the screen.

"Read it."

It was a message from Zin, saying a rumor was circulating about Los Caballeros. It had originated from the DA's office and suggested an impending indictment against not Zin, Brix, and the other current members of Los Caballeros. It didn't stop there. The message also stated my father, his, and Press and Beau's would be indicted as well. The worst of it was Cooley was giving credit solely to the hard work of ADA Seraphina Reeve.

"He's spreading misinformation when she isn't there to negate it."

Press shook his head and turned his computer so he could see the screen as well. "Take a look."

I sighed. "What is this?" I repeated.

"Seraphina's browser history while at Tryst's ranch."

"Come on, Press, you're taking this too far."

"Am I? Check out the dates and times. Is there a reasonable explanation why she would devote so many hours to research Los Caballeros?"

"Boredom? Curiosity? Trying to keep her mind off her sister?"

"This, coupled with Zin's email, requires action, Ridge."

I stood, practically knocking my chair over in doing so. "Come with me," I barked.

Press followed me out one of the building's back doors and over to where I'd seen his SUV parked.

"Where are we going?" he asked.

"Nowhere." I walked to the passenger side and got in when he unlocked the doors. "You said Zin's email, coupled with Sera's browsing history, requires action. What would you have me do, Press?"

"Ask her about it."

"You can't really be suggesting I do that now?"

He started to speak, but shut his mouth.

I rested my head against the seat and let out a deep breath. "Cooley is trying to get a reaction. That's all this is."

"You better be right, my friend."

"Has Zin spoken with Brix about this?"

"He has."

I got out of the vehicle only to realize it was too early in California to place a call. On my way back to the warehouse, I was about to round a corner when I heard a voice that sounded like the terminal operations manager.

"Correct. They're not expecting arrival until tomorrow night." There was a pause followed by the man swearing. "*Fuck off.* Of course I changed the SSA numbers. What kind of bloody wanker does he take me for?" Another pause. "I bought you twenty-four hours to unload. The rest is up to you."

I went around the opposite corner and in the same door Press and I had come out of when it sounded as though the call had ended.

"We need to talk," I said to Gunner and Razor. "Ares, Doc, and Merrigan too."

I was stunned when Gunner didn't ask what about but walked straight over to Doc and Merrigan while Razor went in Ares' direction. Since he was talking to Kodiak at the time, both men followed him to where I waited.

"The ship is arriving early," I said when everyone was assembled. "I overheard the terminal manager say he'd switched the SSA numbers, giving whoever he was talking to an extra twenty-four hours to get everything off-loaded."

"If those receiving this cargo think they have twenty-four hours, it means we can anticipate the ship arriving tonight. Let's get to work. Only those you trust with your *own* life get briefed," said Doc. With his directive, everyone spread out and gathered people into small groups. "You brief your team," Doc said to me.

"Roger that," I responded, walking away like the others had.

Since I saw Merrigan speaking with Seraphina and my brother, I summoned Beau, Snapper, and Kick in a different direction. When Press came in the same door I had, I waved him over too.

"I overheard the terminal manager on the phone," I began. Once I told them everything I'd heard, the five of us dispersed to two of the smaller groups. Snapper and Kick joined Gunner, Razor, and the Shadow Ops guys. Press, Beau, and I walked over to Merrigan.

"How are you holding up?" I asked Seraphina once Merrigan finished her brief and walked away with Dalton to talk to the medical team.

"To be honest, grateful I don't have to wait another thirty hours to see my sister."

"If this terminal operator is dirty, my guess is the one in Altamira is too."

"I agree. If it were my investigation, I'd be looking into terminal operations in Yavaros too."

I had no doubt K19 had already begun the process of checking into both.

"How will we know which ship it is?" she asked.

I pointed to the group speaking with Gunner. "I'm sure they're working it out now."

"How did you find out? Merrigan didn't say other than you overheard a conversation."

"Press and I stepped outside for a few minutes. When I returned, I heard the man on the phone."

"Good thing you did." She paused but kept her eyes focused on mine. "I hope you know I appreciate everything you've done, all that you're doing to help find my sister. While I hope my comment didn't offend you, I spoke the truth. The majority of vigilante groups, if you want to call them that, do more to impede justice than they do help."

"Present company excluded?" I couldn't help but ask.

"Sometimes."

"Sera?" God, what could I say? I couldn't ask her if she planned to continue her pursuit of Los Caballeros, now armed with the evidence she'd need to follow through with her initial threats. I trusted her, for fuck's sake.

"What?"

"Never mind. It wasn't important."

"No, tell me."

"I was going to ask if you wanted me to switch apartments to give you time alone with Luisa once we find her."

She thought about it for several seconds, then nodded. "It would be a good idea if you would."

That quickly, I felt her slipping away from me. The closeness I'd felt when I held her in my arms last night as we slept seemed nonexistent. She was withdrawing. I'd served my purpose, and now she was done with me.

God, why was I such a jackass when it came to women? Alex hadn't done what Seraphina was doing, but there were enough signs for me to know a relationship between us would never last. I'd ignored what my gut knew. This time, I wouldn't be so foolish.

23

Ridge

Unlike the hours that dragged before I'd overheard the conversation about the ship arriving tonight, the next twelve flew by. I disengaged from the victim response team and asked Gunner how I could assist his group instead. He pointed me to Snapper and Kick, who were heading up moving the victims into the triage center once they were out of the containers.

Like Seraphina, I wondered how we'd know which ship to board without involving the terminal operations manager.

"Customs," said Snapper when I mentioned it. "They'll at least know which ships are coming from Altamira. If not there, we'll check every ship arriving from Mexico. At the same time, the K19 crew who remained in Yavaros is leaning heavily on Varilla to give up more information."

Every so often, I'd look over at Sera and catch her looking at me. Each time it happened, her eyes scrunched as though she was asking what was wrong. Or maybe I was misreading that too.

Once this was over, maybe I'd spend some time at Tryst's ranch, exploring why I was such a schmuck when it came to women. I felt certain Brix's uncle would be more than willing to share his opinion on the subject.

I'd also talk to my father and see what in the hell had happened between him and Seraphina's dad. I wanted to head in the opposite direction when I saw Press stalking toward me. If he'd found more evidence of Sera plotting against Los Caballeros, I didn't want him to tell me until after we'd rescued her sister. As it was, it was hard enough for me to be around her.

"I've been chatting with Zin—"

"Save it, Press."

He raised a brow.

"I need to focus on the human traffickers now, not on whether Los Caballeros' existence is being threatened."

"That's just it. After hashing it out with Zin, I don't believe Ms. Reeve would have anything truly damning on us."

"Ms. Reeve? Her name is Seraphina."

Press sighed. "Yes, Ridge. I don't believe Seraphina has anything to pursue on Brix or us. All we really did was facilitate K19's involvement and act as support to them. Cooley won't be able to touch Doc Butler or anyone from his organization."

"I as much as admitted our existence."

"Meaning what? No money exchanged hands. A woman came to you, a friend, and told you her sister was missing. Everything taking place from then on was K19."

In terms of proof, he was right. Other than searching Luisa's room and hacking into her phone records, we'd merely acted as facilitators.

Realizing how little Sera had to go on in terms of obstruction of justice did little to relieve me, though. While believing there was no threat against Los Caballeros offered some solace, the idea Sera would betray my trust left me feeling bereft.

Given there was a race to get the medical teams and supplies in place before the ship's arrival, as well as the teams preparing to storm the containers, I hadn't had time to talk to Seraphina at all.

I checked the time and saw it was getting close to zero one hundred when Ares assembled each team leader and told them to let their group know we were T-minus one hour before the ship would be in its berth.

"What's happening with the terminal operations manager?" I asked.

"In custody and singing like a fucking canary," Gunner responded.

There were eight teams of ten armed and suited up in protective gear. An equal number of people in civilian attire were assigned to each unit. Once the all clear was given, they would move in and start aiding victims.

Sera, along with the rest of Los Caballeros, would be floaters, aiding as needed but, more importantly, on the lookout for Luisa.

"Time to move out," announced Doc, leading the first team out of the warehouse.

Sera was standing beside me, and I put my arm around her shoulders. She turned her body, faced me, and we embraced. "I'm so scared," I heard her whisper.

I stroked her hair, not knowing exactly what to say.

She looked up at me. "Noah?"

"It's all going to be okay." While I could feel her eyes boring into mine, I didn't look into hers.

She rested her head against my chest. "We have a lot to talk about once this is over," she said.

I rested my head against hers. "For now, let's focus on Luisa."

When she pulled away, I let her.

I had been given a comms set similar to the one I'd worn in Yavaros, so I could follow along with what was happening on the ship. Along with that, I'd been given the same over-ear hearing protection everyone else wore.

As Gunner said, the entire terminal had gone completely dark and ear-piercing sirens began blaring through the loudspeakers while the teams moved through the containers, each with a Doppler device for thermal imaging.

"Team three in place," I heard Ares say.

"Four in place," said Cayman.

"One in place," said Doc.

This continued until the first eight units were in position and ready to open the container doors. Since the other two were mid-stack, they took longer to find. It also took longer to move the elevated platforms where they needed to be. Once those team leaders announced they were ready, Gunner issued the command to start opening doors.

While I'd anticipated shouting and some gunfire, I picked up on neither. Instead, one by one, I heard the leaders shouting to stand down.

"Jesus Fucking Christ," I heard Gunner say. "All clear. Get your asses over here."

The victim-assistance teams moved out one by one. Shortly after Gunner's signal, I heard several of the other teams calling out Luisa's name.

"We got her. She's in container three," said Ares right about the same time the sirens went silent and the terminal's lights came on.

"Condition?" I asked through the comms.

"Stable."

"They found her," I said, grabbing Seraphina's hand. We raced to where I remembered the third container's placement to be from the schematic.

"Luisa!" Sera shouted, running over to the woman I recognized from the photos, standing with Beau, who had put a blanket around her and was leading her in Sera's direction.

I stood back, watching the sisters embrace.

"You take them in," I said when Beau motioned me closer. Instead of following, I walked over to the fourth container and peered inside as others were assisting the victims out.

"Good God," said Press, covering his nose and mouth with his hand like I had.

While I could see blankets and piles of garbage, it was the stench from waste that overpowered my senses enough to make me step forward to help a woman who looked as though she might pass out at any moment. With Press on one side and me on the other, we got her off the ship and into the triage center.

Once inside, I saw Dalton kneeling by a cot where Luisa lay. Sera was kneeling too, holding her sister's hand while my brother started an IV. As much as I wanted to go over to them, my job of finding Luisa was finished. There were more victims who needed my help.

It took two hours for us to move those rescued from the containers, into the triage center, and for them to be examined by the intake staff.

There was no mention of the traffickers who had been in the containers with them. It appeared they'd been taken off the ship some other way.

Once things settled down and I couldn't find anyone who needed my help, I walked over to where Doc sat with Ares and Kodiak.

"Is there an arrest count?" I asked.

"Zero," said Gunner, walking up behind me. "The fuckers locked them in. The only trap doors were epoxied shut and painted over on the inside, so there was no way for them to escape."

"How did they breathe?" I asked.

"Fans hooked to car batteries circulated air from somewhere," said Ares. "Teams are processing each of the containers now."

"Others are searching the rest of the ship since the two mid-stack were full of cargo," Gunner added.

I was incredulous. "You're saying the containers were put on the ship with no one guarding them? What if something went wrong?"

"Cost of doing business," Gunner muttered. "I'll send these bastards straight to hell if it's the last thing I do."

It was a miracle there were no losses of life, at least not so far. Although I didn't think there were any victims who'd been classified as *expectant*.

"How's the sister?" Kodiak asked.

I looked over and saw Press and Beau were with Luisa and Seraphina. Dalton had moved on to treat other victims. "Safe," I said since I had no direct knowledge of her condition. "Thank you." I looked from Kodiak to Doc to Ares. "What happens next?" I asked.

"Once a victim receives the necessary medical attention, the reunification team moves in. From there, we'll start taking groups home. We have two more planes headed this way now."

"What about the traffickers?" As soon as I asked, I wondered if maybe I was out of line.

"Gunner and Razor are heading up that effort with Cayman's and Puck's help," said Doc, standing when Merrigan approached. He opened his arms, and she walked into them.

I quietly excused myself, but she called after me.

"I came over to tell you I think Seraphina and her sister are ready to leave if you'd like to return to London."

"Got it. Thanks." While I would prefer to stay here and help where needed, I couldn't keep avoiding her. I was walking in her direction when her eyes met mine. She stood, met me partway, and put her arms around me.

"Come meet my sister," she said after squeezing me so tight.

"I'd like that." I took a step back.

"But first, we need to talk."

I shook my head. "We can talk later. Your sister is most important right now."

Sera looked into my eyes. "Please, Noah."

"Sure. Of course."

The sun was starting to come up when I followed her outside. She stopped and put her arms around me like she had a minute ago, and I did the same.

"I don't know how to thank you, Noah."

"Seeing your sister safe is all the thanks I need."

"What happened? Please don't say nothing. I feel very disconnected from you. If it was my vigilante comment, I already told you I was sorry."

She hadn't, actually. What she'd said was she hoped I wasn't offended. "Everything is fine. We're all mentally and emotionally exhausted. I was on my way to see if you wanted to return to London." I dropped my arms and took a step back.

"Merrigan suggested Malin and Alegria go too, although I don't think Luisa is as fragile as everyone thinks she is."

"That's a good idea. I'll get with Press and see about moving you over to the four-bedroom apartment."

"Not necessary. One of the bedrooms in the apartment we're staying in has two twin beds. Luisa and I can stay in there. That way, if she wakes up in the night or needs anything, I'm with her."

"However you'd be most comfortable."

"Noah?"

"Come on, introduce me to your sister." I took her hand and led her inside, ignoring the way she'd repeated my name.

"Luisa, this is the knight in shining armor I told you about, Noah Ridge," Sera said when we found her sister sitting up on the cot.

"Please don't get up," I said when she shifted to stand. I leaned down and took her outstretched hand.

"Thank you." Her eyes filled with tears, which quickly turned into sobs. I was about to sit down to comfort her when Beau and Press jockeyed to do the same thing. Beau beat his brother and me. What in the hell was that all about?

"They've been this way since they got here," said Sera, putting her arm around me. She rested her other hand on my chest and her head on my shoulder.

"Have you called your mom?" I asked.

"I did, and Luisa spoke with her. She asked me to convey her thanks to you too."

I wouldn't ask, but if I had, I wouldn't at all be surprised if her thanks were collective rather than to me specifically.

Sera let go and sat beside her sister. "Would you like Malin and Alegria to come with us?"

Luisa looked up at me, then at Press. "You're going with us too, right?"

"We can, or we can stay here. Whichever you'd prefer," I offered.

Luisa turned to Beau. "I think I'd be more comfortable, if you don't mind coming with us." She also looked up at Press.

I was about to reiterate I'd stay here when Sera stood and took my hand. Not to mention, I was getting tired of hearing me say it myself.

"Let's go. We could all use some rest," she said.

24

Seraphina

When Beau offered to sit in the very back so Luisa and I could sit together and Noah could sit up front, I had to admit I was disappointed. If he'd been seated in the row behind us, I could've turned around to talk to him. As it was, he hadn't glanced my way once.

Each time I'd put my arms around him, I felt him stiffen, and whereas before, he'd been as demonstrative as I was, now he didn't make a single move to hug me or hold my hand. It had all been me.

It couldn't be my comment about vigilantes. He had to know what I'd said was true. Whether he agreed or not, to pull back like he was doing seemed so out of character. There had to be more to it. Once we were at the apartment and Luisa was settled, I'd talk to him about it.

When I intended to do so an hour after we'd arrived, Press told me Noah had left.

"Where'd he go?" I asked.

"He said something about the hotel."

"Surely not to stay?"

Press shrugged. "I'm not certain."

I returned to the bedroom where Luisa was sleeping, pulled out my phone, and sent him a text. *When will you be back?* I lay on the bed, waiting for him to answer, and drifted to sleep. When I woke an hour later, he still hadn't responded.

I got up and went out to the living room, where Press and Beau still sat.

"Can I get you anything?" Beau asked, standing as soon as I walked in.

"I'm trying to reach Noah."

"He's probably sleeping," said Press, looking up from the book he was reading.

"Oh, is he back?"

"From?"

This conversation seemed as strange as the ones I'd been having with Noah. "The hotel."

"No." Press returned to reading.

"How's Luisa?" Beau asked.

"Asleep. I suppose I should be as well."

"My brother and I will take turns staying here with you and your sister. If you need anything, let one of us know."

Part of me wanted to tell him it was unnecessary. I didn't. What I really wanted was for Noah to be here instead. Was that fair? The man had gotten as little sleep as I had. Maybe less. I could wait until after we'd both had a chance to rest to talk to him.

"If Noah returns, can you please ask him to let me know?" I said to Beau. Out of the corner of my eye, I saw Press look up, raise a brow, then return to his book.

I slept on and off through the night. Whenever I woke, I'd check on my sister, who hadn't woken at all as far as I knew, then see if Noah had responded. He hadn't.

When I went out to make some coffee, Beau was asleep on the sofa.

"Good morning," I heard him say when I was tip-toeing down the hall.

I turned around. "Sorry. I didn't want to wake you."

"It's okay. I'd only closed my eyes for a moment. I slept for a few hours, then switched with Press. I've only been here a few minutes."

"I'm sorry to keep asking, but have you heard from Noah?"

"Yeah. Well, Press did. I guess he returned to Felixstowe to see what else he could do to help. From what my brother said, they're hoping to get two of the planes on their way to the States later today."

"Will we be on one?"

"Definitely."

"Will Noah?"

"I'm not sure."

I could hardly leave my sister, but I sensed something had gone really wrong between Noah and me. "Has he said anything? I mean, about me?"

"Not that I know of."

As Beau had said, Luisa and I were on the plane leaving Heathrow that afternoon. He and Press were too, along with Malin and her husband. Like on our flight from Mexico here, Alegria and her husband were in the cockpit. According to Press, Noah was on the second plane.

My heart sank when he'd said it. More, each time I checked my phone and there was no message from him.

When the plane landed on the beach in front of their house, Press and Beau insisted Luisa and I stay with them at Seahorse. Given I'd be sleeping on the sofa if we stayed at my mom's apartment, I was happy to take them up on it. It was also good for Luisa, who seemed more like herself with every passing hour.

"I'm sure my mom will be anxious to see my sister."

Neither man said a word, but when we deboarded, she was waiting at the bottom of the stairs.

"How are you doing?" I asked Luisa later. She and my mom were sitting on chaise lounges on the deck. "It's a little chilly right by the ocean. Can I get you another blanket?"

Luisa pointed to her left. "Beau brought two more, then Press did too."

"They're so attentive," my mother commented. "Will you be out here for a bit?" she asked, getting up.

"Definitely."

"I might lie down inside if you don't mind."

Luisa hadn't said anything yet about Jorge or what had happened between the time she went missing and when she was rescued from the ship in Felixstowe. While we hadn't been in the States for more than a couple of hours, I knew, soon, she'd need to talk to someone. A counselor definitely, but also to law enforcement. Not that I had any idea who would be handling the investigation. Luisa had disappeared from San Luis Obispo, so my guess would be either the SLO police department or the county sheriff would want to get a statement.

"I should probably check in with my office," I said with a complete lack of conviction. I'd already decided to resign my position with the DA.

Since Noah, whom I hadn't heard from, had covered the cost of my auction bid, I still had ten grand in savings I could live off until I found another law firm to work for. From what I'd witnessed with colleagues who'd left prosecution to work in defense, their experience with Cooley made them highly sought after.

Luisa reached out and took my hand. "What's going on, Seraphina? You seem troubled about more than me."

I turned and looked at her. "I don't want to go back to work."

She smiled. "Who does? Especially after being here."

"The Barrett brothers will definitely spoil you."

"What else is bothering you? I know it's more than work."

"I've been trying to reach Noah Ridge."

Luisa looked out at the ocean. "He's giving us time."

"I know, but I haven't talked to him since we returned to the apartment in London. It feels wrong. Like something is up."

"Have you asked Press or Beau?"

"Both are mum on the subject." I heard the door open and glanced over my shoulder. Beau walked out and joined us.

"Can I get you ladies anything?"

"Nothing for me, thanks," I answered.

"Actually, there is something she needs," said my sister. "Can you arrange to have Noah Ridge delivered?"

Beau chuckled, my sister laughed, and I was mortified. More so when I heard Beau say, "We're fresh out of Noahs, but how about some pizza?"

25

Ridge

I hadn't been at the Eaton Square apartment fifteen minutes before I received a call from Zin and Brix. I didn't realize it was from both of them until I picked up.

"What's wrong?" I asked.

"Cooley got a judge to okay a search warrant for the Los Cab wine caves," said Zin.

"I told him he was overreacting," said Brix. "We have nothing to hide and nothing for them to find. The wine rooms are no different than those in many of the caves in the area, including Butler Ranch."

"What are you worried about, Zin?" I asked. "Obviously something."

"You know about Seraphina Reeve's browser history. You also know Cooley is spreading rumors about indictments being handed down."

"Doesn't it have to start with arrests or depositions or something?"

"Subpoenas," he answered.

"Have one or both of you received one?"

"No," Brix answered first. "And he hasn't, either."

"What do you want me to do?" I asked.

"Press has kept me updated on the search and rescue. He said two planes are returning to the States this afternoon."

"That's right."

"Get back as soon as you can, Ridge."

I ended my call with them and rang Doc, checking on the feasibility of their request.

"We're getting ready to transport a few of these folks to London. What's your twenty?"

"I've been at the apartment about a half hour."

"I hate to ask this, but we could use more vehicles down here."

"On my way."

With the exception of Luisa and five others, the victims were Mexican nationals. When I arrived at Felixstowe, Doc told me they'd decided not to fly both planes to the States. One would return to the San Luis Obispo airfield; the other would take as many as the plane could hold comfortably to Tryst's ranch.

Doc, Merrigan, Razor, and I were scheduled to be on the aircraft going to Alamos. Gunner, Ares, and the rest of the Shadow Ops guys were remaining in England. Snapper and Kick were asked to stay on as well and, according to Doc, help with the investigation. Dalton was staying too but would travel with the rest of the victims as soon as their health was stable enough for the flight.

"You won't be able to get into a room with Snapper and Kick when this is over," said Dalton. "Their heads will be too big."

I'd sent a message to Press before leaving Felixstowe for the second time that day, asking about Seraphina and her sister. He'd responded by saying they were both sleeping. After informing him it didn't look as though I'd be returning to the apartment, I asked him to pick up the bottle of wine I'd arranged to have delivered to the hotel and make sure Seraphina and her sister shared it.

Between when I sent that message and the time I got on the plane, I hadn't had a moment to do more than breathe. Once we were in the air, I slept as soon as I was in my seat. I hadn't woken up once the entire flight, until Dalton nudged me, saying we were about to land.

Tryst, two of Brix's other brothers—Cru and Trevino—along with the people who worked on the ranch, had been busy making arrangements to bring the families of the victims to Alamos. When we landed, it was like a huge welcome-home party—complete with a tent, tables, chairs, and more than enough food and drinks for everyone.

"How are things at Los Cab?" I asked Cru, sitting beside him and Dalton after I'd gotten a plate of food.

"The search was carried out yesterday. Other than a couple of bottles of wine, which they tried to make off with, they didn't find anything."

"There was nothing there to find."

"Zin is freaking out, saying the computers are next."

"Press will take care of that." I took a bite of the freshly made tortilla I'd filled with carnitas.

"I already did it," said Trevino. He was the third youngest of the Avila brothers, and while he was a member of Los Caballeros, he'd taken a step away due to health issues after a recent head injury.

"How are you feelin', Trev?" I asked. It had only been a few weeks since he was knocked unconscious by a couple of meth heads. Brix had been the one to find him in the wine caves, where the two men had lured him.

"I have good days and bad. The migraines are rough."

My eyes met Tryst's.

"I've asked Trevino to remain on the ranch," he said. "There are a few things I could use his help with."

"He's lying," said Trev. "He doesn't need my help. He wants to heal me."

The look that passed between uncle and nephew was full of the kind of love seen between father and son.

"I'll admit I'd give about anything to spend more time here," I said between bites of food. "For the tortillas alone."

"You're needed in San Luis Obispo," said Tryst.

"I know."

"Speaking of being needed at home, as much as we love this place, Merrigan and I are heading to Santa Barbara tonight. Anyone who wants a lift, say the word." Doc looked straight at me.

"Word."

"We aren't leaving for at least another hour, maybe two," said Merrigan, watching as I got up from the table to clear my plate. "You hardly ate anything."

"I guess I'm not as hungry as I thought."

Since I had some time to kill, I walked to the temple and went inside. The last time I was here was with Seraphina. Fuck, I missed her. I sat down in the same pew and said a prayer of thanks to whatever gods or deities she'd prayed to that day.

When the door opened, I knew who it was. "Hey, Tryst," I said without turning around.

"What's on your mind, Noah?" he asked, sitting beside me.

"Seraphina Reeve." I sighed and shook my head. "What is wrong with me?"

Tryst put his hand on my shoulder. "Nothing is wrong with you. What makes you ask such a question?"

"I'm obsessing. The same as I did with Alex."

Tryst shook his head. "There is no comparison."

"You know Zin and Press think she's been gathering evidence on Los Caballeros the entire time we were looking for her sister?"

"What do you believe?"

"I told him she wouldn't do that."

"And?"

"She said a couple of things I can't get out of my head."

"What?"

As I reiterated her words, I could tell he thought I was overreacting. I had to agree.

"In your heart, you know she wouldn't do the things they're accusing her of."

"What about the browser history? It was from her time here, Tryst."

"It proves nothing. Ask her, if you need to."

"I don't know what to do."

Tryst closed his eyes and raised his face to the light coming in through the windows in the steeple. "Of course you do." He got up, and a few seconds later, I heard the temple door open and close.

I sat in the pew for a few more minutes, mulling over Tryst's words. I did know what I needed to do. First, I needed to admit something had come between us. Then I owed Sera the benefit of the doubt. I wouldn't want to be accused of something and not given the opportunity to tell my side of the story.

By the time I got back to San Luis Obispo, it would be after midnight, but it was still early enough for me to call now.

"Noah?" Sera's voice sounded as though she was both groggy and worried.

"Hey, I'm sorry it's taken me so long to get back to you."

"Where are you?" she asked.

"At Tryst's ranch, but I'll be on a plane to the States later tonight. I haven't gotten much sleep the last few days, but I was hoping I could see you tomorrow afternoon."

"Yes, I'd like that. I miss you, Noah."

"I miss you too, Sera."

26

Seraphina

Since I had already planned to go into the office tomorrow morning and hand in my resignation, it was best Noah and I wouldn't see each other until this afternoon.

I dreaded my conversation with William Cooley, but I wanted to get it over with so I could move on with my life.

After sticking my head in the bedroom door to make sure Luisa was still asleep, I went into the kitchen for a glass of water. Press was standing near the French doors leading to the oceanfront deck.

"Everything okay?" he asked, noticing my reflection in the window.

"I wanted some water." I poured a glass and walked over to where he stood. "Thank you for being so kind to my sister and my mom."

"I am happy to do so."

"I'm sure they won't want to overstay their welcome and—"

"I've seen where they live, Seraphina. The neighborhood isn't safe, and the apartment lacks the most basic security."

"Agreed. I've been thinking about getting a place big enough for the three of us to live together. While I can't afford much, if we pool what we've each been paying, we can swing it."

"Doesn't the DA's office compensate you fairly?"

"Fairly, yes. Generously, no." I didn't tell Press I intended to resign since I didn't want him to think I expected the three of us to stay on here indefinitely.

"Your sister will feel safer here."

The man hadn't looked at me once during the entire conversation. His eyes didn't even meet mine in my reflection.

"Press, is there something wrong?"

"Not at all." Still no eye contact.

"Do you have an issue with me specifically? If so, I can leave right now."

He finally turned in my direction. "Your sister needs you. I suggest you consider putting her before yourself."

I wanted to slap his face. I'd done nothing besides put Luisa before myself. How dare he suggest otherwise?

Instead, I said goodnight and returned to the bedroom my sister and I were sharing.

I spent most of the night tossing and turning, unable to sleep. Meeting with Cooley weighed heavily on my mind, but so did Press' attitude toward me. When coupled with my mother's opinion of Noah and his family, I felt like I was living inside a soap opera.

Why was everything so complicated? If my mom would simply be forthright about what had happened between Hewitt Ridge and my family, perhaps misunderstandings could be resolved. As far as Press' treatment of me, if he had an issue, I'd prefer he tell me what it was. The way things were, I felt increasingly uncomfortable staying in his house. However, he was right to say Luisa needed me here with her. Until she didn't, or until she was ready to go home, I'd stay out of Press' way as much as possible.

"Are you sure you have to return to work already?" my mother asked the next morning as I was on my way out.

"I'm only going in for a meeting. I'll be back in a couple of hours. Between you, Press, and Beau, Luisa will have all the support she needs until I return."

"It isn't Luisa I'm worried about. You seem very anxious, Seraphina. Is there something more with your sister's abduction you haven't informed me of?"

I shook my head. "It's been a very tense week, Mom. I'm sure my body hasn't recovered from the adrenaline surge."

"You aren't being honest with me."

It was on the tip of my tongue to accuse her of the same thing. However, now wasn't the time for us to argue. I walked over and kissed her cheek. It dawned on me that my car wasn't here. "I'll be back soon. Um, can I borrow your car?"

"Where are you off to?" Beau asked, walking into the kitchen.

"To my office. I thought it best to check in."

He pulled a key fob out of his pocket and handed it to me. "Take mine. It's the red Audi." Given my mom's rust bucket made me nervous every time I was in it, I accepted his offer. Maybe later, when Noah and I got together, I'd ask him to swing me by my place to pick up mine.

The anxiety my mother had picked up on increased on the half-hour drive from Cambria into downtown San Luis Obispo. The closer I got, the more worried I became over what DA Cooley would say when I told him I was leaving.

I parked Beau's Audi in my assigned space and walked the short distance to the elevator.

"Miss Seraphina, welcome back," said one of the guys at the security checkpoint inside the main door of the courthouse.

"Thanks, Tom," I said when he waved me through.

I took another elevator up to the tenth floor, where my office was.

"Seraphina! We didn't expect you," said the receptionist, Ruth.

"I won't be here long today. Is Mr. Cooley in?"

She started to nod but picked up her phone. "Hello, sir. Ms. Reeve has arrived." She paused. "Yes, sir. I'll send her back."

"He wants to see you."

"Okay, I'll drop my stuff in my office first, then head in."

"You, uh, should go to his office first."

I cocked my head and went left rather than right, ignoring her suggestion. I pulled out my keys to unlock my door, but it wouldn't open.

"The lock has been changed, Ms. Reeve." I nearly jumped when Cooley walked up beside me.

"Why?"

"I asked you to come to my office first."

"Yes, sir," I muttered, following him in the opposite direction and feeling more nauseated with every step I took. He'd obviously been informed I'd gone to Los Caballeros for help to find my sister. I wasn't surprised.

"Take a seat."

The chairs in front of the man's desk were so low I often felt as though my chin fell at his desk's height. It reminded me of being in the principal's office, back when I used to go in to report the other kids bullying Luisa.

"Some disturbing news has been brought to my attention, Ms. Reeve." He paused as if to let me ask about it, but I remained silent. "Very well," he continued.

I watched as he opened a manila envelope on the desk in front of him and pulled out photographs. He spread them out. Not that I could see them from where I sat.

"I'd ask for an explanation, but these speak for themselves."

I stood, and he turned one of the photos around so it faced me. It was of Noah and me at the restaurant in London.

"I wonder what your sister would think, seeing these."

I glanced at the other images spread out on his desk. In each, Noah and I appeared as a happy couple out on a date. In the ones taken on our short walk from the restaurant to the apartment, my arm was tucked in his, and we were both smiling.

When I sat down, he smirked. "I know everything, Seraphina. How you went to them for help, traveled by private plane first to Mexico then to England. How the 'cowboy vigilantes' superseded law enforcement in both countries, and your role in facilitating the crimes they committed."

Everything he'd said was taken out of context, twisted, and misrepresented. I knew better than to speak, though. Not without the attorney I'd be hiring present.

I took the envelope containing my letter of resignation and set it in front of him.

"You should be aware a judge approved a search warrant two days ago for the Los Caballeros property. Further warrants, along with indictments, will be issued in the coming days."

I had nothing to say, so I turned to leave. He had my resignation. There was nothing left to be said. I didn't keep personal things in my office anyway, so there was no need to ask to access it. The only things I'd hung on the wall were my degrees. I could easily obtain copies.

"Before you walk out, you should know I've started proceedings to have you disbarred."

I spun around. "*Disbarred?* On what grounds?"

He smiled. He'd gotten the exact reaction he wanted from me. "You might want to sit back down, Seraphina, and listen to the deal I'm prepared to offer."

27

Ridge

It was a little after noon when I finally woke, still feeling tired but anxious to see Sera. I picked up my phone to send her a message after I'd hit the bathroom and made a cup of coffee. When I swiped the screen, I saw she'd already sent one to me.

Something came up. Unable to meet today.

I called her, but it went straight to voicemail. When I sent a reply, it bounced back, saying it was undeliverable. Next, I called Press.

"I heard you returned last evening," he said.

"More like early this morning, but yes, I'm home."

"How are things in Alamos?"

"The first round of victims have been reunited with their families. I believe another plane is en route now with those whose health prevented them from traveling earlier. Dalton is among those flying with them."

"Have you heard anything about the ongoing investigation?"

"Nothing yet, other than each of the locations where the containers were scheduled to be delivered looked as though they'd been abandoned for decades." I cleared my throat. "Is Sera still at your place?"

"Negative. She left earlier to go to work. Hell of a thing, leaving her sister to return to the cesspool they call the DA's office. Unless, of course, she's working on the indictments Zin said he's heard were about to be handed down."

"So we're innocent until proven guilty, but she's not? What the hell, Press?"

"I'd say there's proof enough. You're biased, my friend."

"Fuck off, Press. If she shows up, please ask her to get in touch with me." I heard Press start to say something, but I ended the call anyway.

I was really sick of hearing about her so-called crimes against Los Caballeros in the same way I was sick of hearing about our own. It was getting to the point where I was considering taking a break, like Trev was, if only to get my head sorted out.

I wouldn't, though. Not now, and maybe never. If there actually were indictments headed our way, I'd stand shoulder to shoulder with the men I considered as close as my actual brother.

Since going to my house on See Canyon Road would only remind me of being there with Seraphina and make me miss her more, I went to Ridge Winery instead. Apart from the tasting room, the rest of the operations were shut down for the season. Ridge employed a viticulturist who worked alongside my dad and me, but there was so little to do in the vineyards this time of year, I doubted the man spent more than an hour each day spot-checking the various varietals.

I was about to pull through the gates when a familiar-looking car drove up next to me. "Hey, Alex," I said when she waved and rolled her window down.

"Hey, Ridge-man. Heard you were back in town."

"I'm surprised you heard I was gone."

"You were at my uncle's ranch. I'm not that out of touch with my family. Where are you headed?"

"Thought I'd go for a ride."

"Want some company?"

"You're telling me you have time to throw a leg over?"

"No, but I will talk to you while you get Quasimodo saddled up. Are you still riding him?"

"Sure am."

"Lead the way."

I pulled through the gates, and Alex followed. There was a time her being here would've made me happier than I was. Now, though, I wished it was Seraphina who'd met me at the gate.

"Brix mentioned SLO PD searched the caves."

"I heard. Cru said one of them tried to make off with a couple bottles of wine."

"I hadn't heard about that." She pulled a stool over and sat on it. "Tell me what's goin' on with you and the ADA."

"That's complicated, Alex."

"Zin says she has an ulterior motive."

"Did the caballeros get a new member while I was out of town?"

"I've been honorary my whole life. You know that."

I raised a brow. I'd also heard she got in a world of hurt when her father caught her spying on one of the meetings.

"Whatever. I know, okay? There's no point in denying it. Now, what's up with you and Seraphina Reeve? Oh, and thanks for the bonus you tacked onto the bid for the kids, but I have to ask. Why didn't she pay it herself? Did you have it fixed like Brix?"

If I had, it sure wouldn't have been Sera I would've chosen to win. At least not then.

"It's complicated," I repeated.

"Do you think she's really on the hunt?"

"For?"

"C'mon, don't make me work this hard."

I pulled a stool over and sat beside her. "You wanna know the truth?"

"Of course I do."

"I'm crazy about her. First time since...you know."

"I'm happy to hear it." I was used to the hesitation in Alex's voice.

"But you, like everyone else, think she has an ulterior motive."

"You guys rescued her sister."

I shook my head. "Is there anything you don't know?"

"One thing."

"Let's hear it."

"Why don't you ask her, Ridge?"

I rested my elbows on my knees and looked down at the ground. "I plan to. Or maybe it's planned now."

"What's that mean?" Alex asked.

"We were supposed to get together this afternoon. She canceled, saying something came up."

"Hmm." She tapped her bottom lip like Tryst so often did. "Where is she now?"

"According to Press, she went to her office."

"You can't exactly show up there and invite her to lunch. Her sister is staying at Seahorse, though, right?"

"I'm beginning to think you're clairvoyant."

She nudged me with her knee. "Nah, just nosy. Anyway, camp out there until she gets back, then ask her straight out."

I shook my head. "I can't do that."

"Why not? Then you'll know."

"Like you said, her sister is at Seahorse, recovering. If I show up there and Sera doesn't want to see me, then I've made it uncomfortable for everyone."

Alex raised a brow. "Vader said something about her hating it when people call her Sera. Maybe that's why she's avoiding you."

"I call her Sera; she calls me Noah."

I looked up at Alex when she didn't say anything for longer than she usually went without talking.

"You're in love with her, aren't you?"

I shrugged and stood. "Quasimodo isn't going to saddle himself."

"You sure named him right. That's the butt-ugliest horse I've ever seen."

"Hey, now. Be nice. Besides, you can get in big trouble with the cancel culture for not being sensitive to my horse's appearance."

"You are so full of shit. You don't even know what cancel culture is. By the way, it's a *thing,* not an *it.*"

"Whatever. See ya, Alex."

She walked over and scratched Quasi between his ears. "Give me a hug before I go, Noah."

I shook my head and held my arms open. "Only Sera gets to call me Noah."

"And your mom."

28

"Goddamn motherfucker," I muttered under my breath as the elevator door opened in the parking garage. I hit the key fob to unlock my car at the same time the door of the car next to it opened and a woman got out. Not just any woman—Alex Avila-Butler.

I'd had my fill of dogs with bones in the last three days. Cooley was enough for an entire kennel. Not that Alex was in the parking lot waiting for me. It wasn't like we really knew each other.

I walked the rest of the way to my car, intending to ignore her, when I heard her say my name.

I turned around. "Oh, hi, Alex."

"Don't pretend you didn't see me."

"I saw you. I didn't think you knew my name."

"I know a lot more than that."

I glanced up at the security cameras. The last thing I needed was Cooley's goons seeing me talking to her. I was having a hard enough time navigating the shark-infested waters of the DA's office as it was.

"Sorry. No comment."

She didn't look directly at the camera, thankfully, but she'd seen me do it.

"Do you know if that coffee place is in this block or the next?" she asked.

I shook my head. "I heard they went out of business."

"Damn. I could really use the caffeine. Guess I'll have to settle for a glass of wine instead. The Mustard Seed is still open, right?"

"I don't know. But why would you go there when you own your own tasting bar?"

"Good point. Okay, take care, Seraphina. Nice to see you."

"You too."

Either I was crazy, or Alex and I had agreed to meet at the wine bar she owned in Cambria.

I got in my car and drove off before she'd started hers. My hands were shaking, and I felt sick to my stomach, knowing I was about to take a dive off the tightrope I'd been walking.

I wouldn't put it past Cooley to have me followed, nor would it surprise me if my cell phone was bugged. He'd probably found a way to hack into it too, which is why I'd blocked everyone's number except Press' and Beau's.

The former had made it clear he had no intention of letting me put him in the middle of Noah and me. Which meant I didn't need to worry about him sending a message on the subject. I'd asked him and his brother to only contact me if my sister or mom needed anything. Whether they'd picked up on why or not, didn't matter.

Regardless, I couldn't risk being followed to Cambria, so when I reached the turnoff for Seahorse, I took that instead and waited until I was sure Alex had followed before pulling in. The gate closed right behind me, but seconds later, I saw it reopen to let her in.

"Seems like you're runnin' from the law, girlfriend," Alex said, getting out of her car after she'd parked next to me. She couldn't have hit the nail more squarely on the head. "Do you think you're being followed?"

"It wouldn't surprise me. If you're here about the payment for the auction—"

She held up her hand. "Stop right there. That isn't why I'm here, and Ridge already took care of it."

My cheeks flamed in embarrassment. I wasn't only too poor to run in the same circles as Alex and her friends, but William Cooley was doing his level best to make sure if I didn't do his bidding, I'd never practice law again.

"I'd invite you inside, but this isn't my house."

"Let's take a walk on the beach."

While she was in shorts, I was in a dress and heels. "I'll meet you out front in a few minutes."

She looked me up and down. "I'll be down the way. By the Pulpit."

The rock she was referring to was right on the other side of Press' property line. While I didn't doubt he still had security monitoring the area, maybe Alex knew something I didn't.

I raced inside, took off my work clothes, and put on a pair of sweats and a T-shirt. I grabbed tennis shoes, but I'd go barefoot on the beach anyway. "I'm going for a walk," I said to my mom and sister, who were sitting in the living room. "I need to blow off some steam before I attempt being human."

"See you in a bit, baby," said my mom. Luisa waved.

I raced down the beach and around the bend where Alex sat waiting. Now that I was here, I had no idea why I'd been so anxious to meet her, other than I didn't want Cooley to know I was, any more than I wanted Press to.

"You're a stress mess," she said when I walked up.

"Thanks."

She shrugged. "Let me see if I've got this right. Cooley is tailing you, and Press is eavesdropping on your every word."

"I doubt he's the only one eavesdropping."

"Did you leave your phone at the house?"

"Yes."

"Good girl." Alex motioned for me to sit on one of the rocks. "So, tell me what's going on."

I shook my head. "I can't."

"What's Cooley got on you?"

I looked out at the ocean. "My livelihood."

"I see." She tapped her lower lip. "I'm going to ask you a question I really hope you'll answer."

I knew what she was going to say, and the truth was, I was working night and day to find out what evidence Cooley had collected and figure out if it was enough to truly go after Los Caballeros or anyone affiliated with it. Which included me, of course.

I looked over at her. "If I can, I will. I might not know the answer."

She shook her head. "Oh, you know it."

"O-o-okay. Shoot."

"Are you in love with Noah Ridge?"

29

Ridge

I'd just sat down on the deck after a long day spent working on my new house when I heard footsteps behind me. "Tryst! I wasn't expecting you," I said when he walked through the patio door. "How'd you get in?"

"The garage was open."

"Seriously? Shit. Let me go close it." It wasn't the first time my brain had short-circuited in the last week.

"I did already."

"What brings you here? I didn't know you were coming to town. I hope I'm not the reason you came all the way up here."

"Only one of the reasons."

"Look—"

He shook his head. "Ask me if I'd like a glass of wine first."

I chuckled. "You got it. Red or white?"

"I left a bottle on the table you can open."

There wasn't much in my house yet, except a small refrigerator, a folding table, and a couple of chairs. There wasn't even a functional bathroom. The construction guys had a porta-potty by the garage I used.

I pulled the wine key out of my back pocket and opened the bottle of rosé Tryst had brought with him. I recognized it as soon as I walked in. It was made by Demetrius, the name of the winery as well as the estate Alex and her husband owned.

"One of my favorites," I said, bringing a glass out to Tryst. "Thank you."

"I stopped to see my niece on my way here."

"Yeah?"

"She told me a very interesting story. Two actually. The first was something she learned only yesterday from her mother—about my brother and Stanley Cooley."

"Any relation to the district attorney?"

Tryst nodded. "His father."

I shook my head when Tryst finished telling me what Alex's mom had told her, but before I could react, he brought up the situation between Sera's mother and my father.

"Have you spoken with him yet?" he asked.

"I still think it's best to wait until my parents are home."

"I disagree. It stands between Seraphina and you."

"There's more standing between us." I hadn't seen or spoken to Sera since we returned to London. "Is this the second story, Tryst? Are you finally going to tell me what you think happened?"

"I can't tell you, because I don't know."

"Maybe it's as simple as Leah deciding my father didn't pay enough for the Reeve place. I know my dad, and I'm sure he was more than fair."

Tryst shook his head. "There's more to it."

"But you don't know what?"

"Call your father."

It was after four here, which meant nine in the morning in Australia. I couldn't use the time of day as an excuse.

"Noah! How nice to hear from you. Your mother and I were talking about you and Beau Barrett. You know Daphne's in California, right?"

Daphne had been Press' brother's childhood sweetheart, and I had no idea she was in the States, let alone California. I wondered if Beau knew.

"I had no idea. I've been out of the country. How's the trip, Dad?"

"We always enjoy our time with the Cullens."

"I hate to interrupt your vacation, but there's something I need to ask you about."

"You sound troubled. What is it?"

"Can you tell me everything that went down when you bought the Reeve property?" My father was silent long enough that I wondered if the call had dropped. "Dad?"

"I'm here. Is there a reason you're asking about this now?"

"I'm friends with Seraphina Reeve, and to be honest, her mother isn't a big fan of mine. We both believe it relates to whatever happened then."

"It does, Noah."

30

Seraphina

Since the day I met Alex on the beach, I'd taken to stopping at my apartment after work each day before going to Seahorse. It gave me time to wind down, so when I did see my mom and sister, I could put on enough of a brave face that they wouldn't know how much of a disaster my life had turned into. I limited myself to a half glass of wine after I'd changed out of my work clothes, turned on music, put my feet up, and closed my eyes.

It had been nine days since we left London and returned to the US. My sister had good days and not-so-good days, but she was gradually improving due, in part, to the counselor Press had hired for her. The woman had been to the house every day, and when she left, my sister was usually in better spirits than before she arrived.

It was only one of the things I'd forever be indebted to Press Barrett for. Not that he'd ever accept thanks from me. He tolerated me for my sister's sake. Nothing beyond.

I still wondered whether it had been wise to tell Alex exactly what was happening behind the closed doors of the DA's office. However, the woman was as relentless as she was good at getting people to spill their guts to her.

Of everything I'd confessed to Alex, the hardest was my feelings for Noah. Yes, I was in love with him. Head over heels. However, until I could find a way to end the DA's obsession with bringing down Los Caballeros, I couldn't see or talk to him. I'd had a hard enough time convincing Cooley there was no way I could get my sister or my mother to leave Seahorse. He'd finally given in, tasking me with gathering as much dirt on the Barretts as I could while I was there.

I knew the hamster wheel I was on with my boss couldn't continue. There were only so many times I could swear on my own life I hadn't found incriminating evidence on Press or the other members of Los Caballeros. Not that I'd confirmed there were actual members. Or that I was indebted to every one of them for rescuing my sister.

Every day, I pretended to be searching for evidence while, at the same time, working my tail off to find what Cooley had on them. It had to have been something to get a judge to sign off on a search warrant. Either that, or the judge was as dirty as the DA.

Soon, though, the tenuous hold I had on my job would slip away, and I'd find myself disbarred or, worse, in jail on the same trumped-up charges Cooley intended to use to take down Los Caballeros.

While I knew without any doubt the reason he had it in for them was personal, I hadn't been able to find a single justification for it.

I'd just finished the last of the wine in my glass when I heard a knock at the door. I considered pretending I wasn't here, but my music was turned up too loud for me to get away with it. Maybe it was one of my neighbors about to ask me to turn it down.

I checked the peephole, spun around, and rested my back against the door. What was Noah doing here? Alex swore to me she wouldn't tell him anything I'd confessed to her, including my feelings, and I'd been stupid enough to believe her.

I pulled open the door and was about to tell him to go away when he pulled me outside, closed my door, and put two fingertips on my lips. He opened the palm of the other hand. In it was a small black wand, no more than five inches long and less than an inch in diameter. He gave it to me. "Wave it around," he whispered into my ear, motioning up and down, back and forth with his arm. He opened the door and gave me a push inside. My place wasn't very big, so it didn't take long to walk its perimeter. Every few feet, a red light would come on, then go off. I did this twice and, when the red light didn't appear again, opened the front door.

Noah took the device from my hand, flipped it over, pressed a button, then nodded. "We can go in."

"What the hell was that all about?"

He pressed the same button he had outside. "See this?"

On the tiny screen, I saw the numbers two and seven. "Yeah?"

"Two cameras, seven listening devices."

I twisted around, trying to remember where the red light had gone on. When I couldn't recall exactly, I held up the middle fingers of both hands and spun in a circle.

Noah put his hand on my wrist and smiled. "They're all dead now."

"Why didn't you tell me before I zapped them? That motherfucker. He's been *watching* me?" The idea of the slimy bastard watching me undress made my skin crawl. "Cooley hired the guy who took photos of us in London."

"I know."

I put my hands on my hips. "As mad as I am at my boss, I'm also really pissed at Alex. How dare she?"

"Alex? What does she have to do with anything? I mean she has something to do with something, but not this."

I cocked my head, trying to make sense of what Noah had said. "She has something to do with something?"

Noah smiled. "Sorry. I'll explain. I promise. But for now, don't be mad at Alex."

"She's the only one I told."

"I found out from someone else."

"Who?"

"Before I answer that, come here." He grabbed my wrist, pulled my body flush with his, and cupped my cheek. "I have missed you so much." He leaned down and kissed me. Once. Quickly. But it was a kiss. "Is this okay?" he asked.

I shook my head, but before he could pull away, I put my hand on the back of his neck and kissed him. I pressed my tongue against his lips, and he opened his mouth to mine. Rather than remaining passive, Noah's kiss was demanding, his breathing ragged. When his hand slid down my back to my ass, I pressed against him on my own. Noah brought his other hand up to my neck, holding me as his mouth made love to mine. "I missed you," he said again, scattering kisses across my jawline and down the side of my neck.

"Wait," I gasped when I felt his hands on the buttons of my shirt.

He rested his forehead against mine. "Sorry. I got carried away."

"Don't apologize. I want this as much as you do."

"But first…"

"Yes. First, we have a lot to talk about. Are you sure it's safe to do it here?"

"Give me your keys."

"To my car?" I asked.

"Yes."

When I handed them to him, he went out the patio door and set them under a pot that he placed right on the edge of the concrete. Then he sent a text to someone.

"What was that all about?"

"A friend is leading the guy who's been following you on a wild goose chase."

"Who's this friend? Alex?"

He laughed and shook his head. "You haven't met her yet. Her family and my family have been friends for years. She's visiting from Australia. Oh, and she's Beau Barrett's girlfriend. She looks more like you than Alex does."

I doubted that was a compliment, since Alex was tall, thin, and could have been a model. Actually, maybe she had been.

"*Wait.* Beau's girlfriend?"

"More like childhood sweetheart, but yeah. I'm pretty sure when she's here, they pick up where they left off. Why?"

"I'm afraid my sister has developed a crush on him. He's been so…But then so has…" I shook my head. "It doesn't matter. Luisa is in no position to develop a crush on anyone. It's just transference anyway. Both Beau and Press have been so good to her. I'll never make it up to them. Or you, for that matter." I looked around my apartment, wondering if I'd be able to set foot in it again without feeling as though I was being watched.

"Ready?" Noah asked.

"Uh, sure. Where are we going?"

"I'd take you to my place on See Canyon Road, but you've already been there. It isn't any different than the last time."

"Noah, as much as I'd like to spend time with you, I really need to go to Seahorse."

He shook his head. "I stopped there first. Your mother *and Press* assured me Luisa was fine. When I asked her directly, she asked me to please not let you come up there tonight."

"Tonight? I can't be gone all night. She needs—"

Noah stopped me with a kiss. A toe-curling, panty-melting, heart-stopping kiss.

"I wouldn't mind returning to See Canyon," I said when he pulled away and looked into my eyes.

"Are you hungry?" he asked once we were in his car.

I nodded, wishing I wasn't but knowing if I didn't eat soon, I'd get cranky.

"Good."

I was confused when he drove straight to his house without stopping at either a store or a restaurant.

"I was hoping you'd say you wanted to come here," he said when he pulled into the garage and the door closed behind his car.

"I'm warning you. If you don't have anything to eat here…"

When he raised a brow, I stopped talking.

He opened the door to the house, turned around, and told me to close my eyes. "Watch your step," he said, taking me by the hand. "Okay, you can open them."

Outdoor patio lights were strung from rafter to rafter, illuminating the space where a rounded sofa made of rattan with cushions on top was placed so it faced the view of the ocean. There were two rounded seats set on each side and a round ottoman, made of the same rattan topped with a cushion.

"Have a seat, and I'll be right back." Noah left the room, but came back a minute later carrying a tray. When he set it on the ottoman, I saw it held wrapped sandwiches, a variety of fruit, and two wineglasses. "Red or white?" he asked.

"Is this an Italian sub?" I asked, pointing.

"Two of them. I also have a Greek salad in the fridge, if you'd prefer that."

I smiled. "Red please, and when did you get a fridge?"

He opened the bottle, poured two glasses, and sat beside me. "Tryst came to visit. He insisted on outfitting the place with a few things."

"Like a refrigerator?"

"And a makeshift bathroom." He patted the seat. "And this. If you put it all together, it makes a bed." Noah unwrapped one of the subs and handed it to me.

"Where do you get these? I love them," I said, taking a big bite.

"Soto's. Do you know of it?"

"In Cambria? You drove all the way up there to get these?"

Noah shook his head. "They opened another location in Pismo."

"That's a little closer, at least."

After we'd eaten our sandwiches and some of the fruit, Noah set the tray on the floor, stood, and poured us each more wine. Before he sat down again, he scooted both of the chairs over.

"Put your legs on the ottoman," he said, pushing the four pieces until they formed a circle.

I rested against the pillows behind me. "This is heavenly." I raised my glass in the direction of the water. "The views, I mean, I've always loved this view. Although I've never been this comfortable when I was looking out at it."

"Are you warm enough?"

I rubbed my arms. "I'm fine."

He put his hand under both my legs, raised them, then moved the ottoman's cushion to the side. He reached in and pulled out a blanket, then set my legs down before covering me with it.

"I can share," I said when he sat beside me. I unfolded it and draped half over him.

Noah put his arm around me and ran his fingers through my hair when I snuggled up against him.

"We have a lot to talk about, Sera."

"I know."

"There are a couple things I want to get straight first."

I shifted to move away, but he held me close to him.

"One, I trust you. Two, I'd give anything to spend every night like this. Until I get more furniture and maybe walls. In other words, I want to be with you, Seraphina."

"I want to be with you too."

"Now that we've gotten those two things out of the way, tell me what's been going on with you and the DA."

"You mean the one who put cameras and bugs in my apartment?"

"One and the same."

"He blackmailed me," I admitted.

"I figured he had."

"He threatened to get me disbarred if I didn't tell him everything that happened in Mexico and England. After I did, he wasn't too happy with me."

"He wasn't?"

"He could hardly go after someone—collectively—who is working with the US and UK governments, MI5, and customs and immigration. Not to mention a private intelligence firm that works almost exclusively with the CIA."

He raised a brow.

"Merrigan helped me with some of that." I groaned. "God, I bet Cooley knows she did. She'll be subpoenaed next. Now I feel terrible."

"She won't be. I guarantee it."

"Well, anyway, I've spent the last few days trying to find out what he has on Los Caballeros that made the judge issue the search warrant."

"Nothing. The judge is as dirty as the DA is."

"I'd considered the possibility." I turned so I could look at him. "How do you know they both are? Do you have proof?"

Noah nodded. "And a motive."

31

Ridge

It took a team effort, like most things did, but between Tryst, Press, Alex, and myself, we'd finally pieced together why William Cooley had made it his life's mission to take down Los Caballeros.

The way Tryst told it, Alex had taken her and Maddox's baby, Coco, to her mom's house. While there, she'd mentioned how the DA, William Cooley, had been granted a search warrant for the wine caves. Alex warned her mother there was a chance he'd try to obtain one to search the house as well.

"That man," she'd said, shaking her head.

"What about him, Mom?"

"First, his father. Now him."

"Alex asked her to elaborate, and what her mother said, explains everything," I told Sera, whose eyes were open wide.

"What happened?"

"It all began when immigration officers showed up at Alex's family's winery and raided the vineyards and arrested several of Alfonso's workers. As you can imagine—well, maybe you didn't know him—but Alex's father had quite a temper. Rather than risk getting on the wrong side of US Immigration, he called a meeting of Los Caballeros."

I continued the story the same way it was told to me, not leaving out any possibly incriminating details—either I trusted Sera or I didn't.

Alfonso, my father, and Press and Beau's father, along with the seven other then-members, started looking into why ICE believed the workers were in the country illegally. They eventually discovered the visas obtained for the workers had been filed fraudulently.

"This made Alfonso angrier since he'd helped every one of the workers arrested and deported, paying for their visas as well as sponsoring any who wanted to become US citizens."

"Let me guess. The attorney was Cooley's father?" said Sera.

"Yep, and it got pretty ugly. A thirty-three-count indictment was handed down by a federal grand jury. Cooley and his law partner were convicted on all the charges against them, which ended up also including money laundering."

"How did this get buried?"

"Well, one of the recipients of the money Alfonso paid Cooley was the governor of California."

Sera's eyes opened wider still. "He *pardoned* them?"

I nodded. "And sealed the records, from the indictments to the conviction to the sentencing. Every bit of it."

"That *sonuvabitch*."

I wasn't sure which *sonuvabitch* Sera was referring to, but it applied to them all.

"If Cooley's father was pardoned, why is he carrying this vendetta? Not to mention, Alfonso Avila did nothing wrong."

"Stanley Cooley—the DA's father—served five years in federal prison before he was pardoned. He wasn't permitted to practice law ever again, and the family was disgraced."

"How old was William at the time? Do you know?"

"Eighteen."

Sera got up and walked over to the windows. "He became an attorney to avenge what happened to his father."

"In part, at least."

When she turned around, her face had gone ashen.

I stood too and walked over to her. "What's going on?"

"It's the same thing I did," she said.

"What do you mean?"

"After my father's accident, our family was buried under a mountain of debt both for medical expenses and a court battle with the family of the four people he'd killed. We lost the only thing we had left, our house, and poor Luisa was bullied every single day by the kids she went to school with, for being the child of a murderer. I decided to become a lawyer out of necessity. I never dreamed it was what I would do when I grew up."

"It isn't the same, Sera. You said it yourself. You did it out of necessity, not because you wanted to avenge your father. You wanted to save the rest of your family."

She nodded, but I could tell she wasn't entirely convinced.

"You're nothing like Cooley," I said when I realized what was really bothering her.

"Aren't I? Do you know what I've been doing at work over the last few days? Trying to find whatever evidence Cooley has on Los Caballeros. Once I did, my intention was to tell you what it was. More, to figure out a way to bury it, or negate it, or something. Regardless, it would have been illegal."

"Have you found anything?"

"No, but the point is—"

"The point is you don't know you would've acted illegally. My guess is when you were actually faced with it, you wouldn't have been able to do it."

"I'm not so sure."

"I am. Would you like to know why?"

She nodded.

"Because even when we were searching for Luisa, you never lost sight of the law. Your belief in the law remained steadfast."

She raised a brow. "What are you talking about?"

"What you said about Los Caballeros *believing* we were the good guys? I can't speak for anyone else, but it resonated with me. To be perfectly honest, at times, I considered taking a break."

Her eyes bored into mine, but she didn't speak.

"It's a slippery slope, isn't it? But neither of us is like Cooley. Neither of us has broken laws because of a personal vendetta. Neither of us has tried to ruin the lives of the innocent. Cooley, on the other hand, sought to destroy Brix's life and the lives of as many of us as he could. And what about you? He's threatening you with disbarment if you don't help him do it."

Sera and I spent the next couple of hours debating how to go after Cooley and what evidence we had to start an investigation.

It was almost one in the morning when Sera looked up from her computer. "I have an idea. It would be up to the Internal Affairs Division of the Fourth Judicial District Attorney's Office to look into the allegations."

"Okay."

"One of the women who left the DA's office became an investigator with the Fourth. Given she already knows Cooley, I can approach her. Worst-case scenario is she doesn't think we have enough to go on."

"You don't think she'd let Cooley know what we're up to?"

Sera shook her head. "Not a chance. She was *fired;* she didn't simply leave. I'd be willing to bet the DA expected her to do the same things he expected of me." She yawned and stretched her arms over her head. "I need to call it a night."

"I'll take you home."

"Home?"

"Or to Seahorse."

She shook her head.

"No? So, uh…"

Sera pointed to the daybed. "I'd prefer to sleep right there."

I pulled her into my arms. "There's something else I'd really like to do."

"Oh, yeah?"

"Tomorrow is Saturday, right? So you don't have to go to the office."

"I'm not sure I would anyway, but why?"

"I'd like to take you out for breakfast."

32

Seraphina

The next day, Noah took me to Huck's in Pismo Beach, the same place we'd met the morning my mom first told me my sister was missing. It felt like a lifetime ago.

"What sounds good to you?" Noah asked.

"I always get the same thing. I love their Cajun omelet."

He smiled and shook his head.

"What?"

"It's the same thing I always order. The last time I ate here—which was after the guys and I went surfing, not the morning I met you—I wondered if you liked spicy food."

"You thought about me?"

Noah slid out of the opposite side of the booth, sat next to me, and picked up his menu.

"What was that all about?"

"When I think about you, I always wish you were beside me."

"I always wish you were beside me too."

He shook his head and took a sip of coffee. "Let me ask you something."

"Okay."

"What happens when Cooley gets kicked out of office?"

"What do you mean?"

"Who takes his place?"

I shrugged. "That's up to the county commissioners. They'll appoint either an interim or permanent replacement. Permanent until the next election, of course."

"Would you want the job?"

Noah's question stunned me. All I'd thought about over the last several days was how soon I could get out of there. "I don't know."

"You'd be good at it."

I smiled. "You don't know I would be. You're just saying that because you kinda like me."

"Kinda?" He draped his arm across the back of the booth. "It's way beyond kinda, Sera."

"It is for me too."

He leaned forward to kiss me when we heard someone clear her throat. "Sorry to interrupt, kids, but I've got two Cajun omelets for ya."

"Thanks, Barb," said Noah, quickly kissing my cheek.

We both dove into our meals, but Noah's question about whether I'd want Cooley's job raced through my mind. I was the lead ADA, so I'd most likely be named interim—if I was still there. I'd have to clean house, no doubt about that. There were few there I would feel comfortable working with, knowing someone had put two cameras and several bugs in my apartment and the same person or someone else had monitored my actions and conversations.

"You're thinking about it, aren't you?"

I put my head on Noah's shoulder and smiled. "I am." My phone rang, and as much as I wanted to ignore it, there were several reasons I hadn't silenced it. "I should take this," I said when I saw my mom was calling.

"Your sister is having a very bad morning. Last night too," she said after I stepped outside to take her call.

"I'll be there in twenty minutes," I said before going back inside, hoping Noah wouldn't mind having to leave right away.

"I need to get to Seahorse. My sister…" I started to cry and couldn't continue.

"What's happened?" he asked, taking my hand in his.

"She had a bad night."

He nodded, took out his wallet, and threw a couple of bills on the table.

"Are you sure you don't want to finish?" I pointed at his food.

"Positive. C'mon, let's get you up there."

I hugged my stomach on the way. This was my fault. I shouldn't have stayed with Noah last night. No matter how many times she told me she was okay, I knew she wasn't. How could she be?

Noah reached over and rubbed my shoulder. There was no doubt he knew what I was thinking, and I appreciated him not trying to talk to me about it.

I raced into the house after the light above the door turned green.

"Where is Luisa?" I asked Press, who met me in the hallway.

"Out on the deck. She's—"

I didn't bother listening to what he said. I needed to see my sister, not have someone who hardly knew her tell me how she was.

"Hey," I said, sitting on the chaise beside her. Tears were rolling down her cheeks. I leaned forward, and we hugged. "I'm sorry I wasn't here last night." I stroked her hair. "Can you tell me what's going on?"

"I'm an idiot. A stupid idiot."

I pulled back and cupped her cheek. "We both know that isn't true. What's this all about?"

"First Jorge. My God, I fell for a fucking human trafficker just because he paid attention to me."

"And second?"

She cried harder and shook her head. My guess was finding out Beau had a girlfriend was the reason for this tailspin. It wasn't about Beau, though. It was about the tenuous hold Luisa had on her life right now. Both Beau and his brother had been "paying attention" to her, the same way Jorge had. They'd invited her to stay in their home, and her sense of safety and security was dependent on them and on me.

"How about a walk on the beach?"

Luisa shook her head. "I want to go home. I don't want to stay here anymore."

"I understand, sweetie. I really do, but the apartment is, well, it isn't in the best neighborhood, and there isn't any kind of security system. I'm not sure you'd feel safe being there."

"I don't want to be here."

"Give me a few minutes to figure this out, okay?"

I saw my mom standing by the French doors, looking out at us.

"She's insisting we leave," she said when I came inside.

"I know. That's what she told me too. Can you sit with her while I see what I can do?"

"Your sister…"

"Mom, please. Go sit with her."

She nodded and went out the doors.

Noah was in the kitchen, talking with Press. "She wants to go home," I said. "While I don't think it's a good idea, I can't force her to stay somewhere she doesn't feel comfortable."

"I have another idea," said Noah.

"I'm open to any suggestions."

"Doc's parents have a ranch adjacent to Los Caballeros. Ridge is two doors down."

"She doesn't know them."

"Actually, she does," said Press. "She's friends with one of Doc's sisters."

"Jada Yáñez lives near Butler Ranch too," Noah added.

"Does Doc's sister still live at home?" I asked.

"No, but Jada does," said Noah. "The thing about staying at Butler Ranch is their security system is as tight as Seahorse's. Laird and Sorcha Butler are also about the nicest people who ever lived."

"I've met them a few times."

"So you know what I mean." Noah put his hand on my shoulder. "Run it by her and see what she thinks."

I nodded.

"She cannot return to that apartment," said Press, looking out the window.

"I agree it isn't ideal, but it's also her home." If Luisa wouldn't go along with staying at Butler Ranch, there might not be an alternative. At least until I could find another place for her, my mom, and me to live.

"They have two guesthouses next door to each other on the property, so all three of you could stay there. I know at least one has three bedrooms."

"Are Laird and Sorcha okay with this?" I asked.

"They are," Noah answered.

I joined my mom and sister outside and presented the idea to them.

"It's your sister's decision," said my mom.

"Luisa?"

"When can we leave?" she asked.

"I would think right away."

"Okay." She got up to go inside.

"Did she tell you what happened?" my mom asked.

"I have a feeling it had something to do with Beau Barrett, and before you say anything, I don't think it's what this is really about. Luisa needs to feel in control of her own life. At the same time, she's more fragile than she appears. My plan is to respect her wishes as best I can while, at the same time, keeping her grounded."

"I appreciate all you do for us, baby."

I hugged her. "I know you do, Mom."

33

Ridge

"I wish she'd stay here," said Press when Sera went outside.

"Butler Ranch is the perfect alternative."

"I know." He shook his head.

"I get it, Press. Your protector instincts are on high alert, and it's hard to turn it off."

"I wish my brother's were," he muttered.

"Beau didn't do anything wrong."

Press shrugged. "Luisa responded to him. He could've been more sensitive."

I disagreed, but there was no point in arguing about it.

"She's here."

"If you mean Daphne, yeah, I know. She and Beau helped me with something late yesterday afternoon."

"I mean here at Seahorse."

"Again, Press, Beau did nothing wrong, and neither did Daphne."

"And yet, Luisa is leaving."

"She'll be safe at Butler Ranch, and you know it. Besides, there aren't two more nurturing people than Laird and Sorcha."

The French doors opened, and Luisa came inside. Sera and her mom followed a minute later.

"My mom is helping get Luisa's things together. My sister has agreed with your suggestion." She turned to Press. "Thank you for everything you've done for my sister. I can never repay your kindness."

My eyes met Press', and I cocked my head.

"Right," he said to me before looking at Sera. "You are more than welcome, and there is nothing to repay. Your sister's well-being is all I care about."

I cleared my throat.

"Right," he repeated. "Would you excuse us?" Press said to me.

"Sure. I'll be in the other room." I sincerely hoped Press was offering Sera the apology I'd told him she deserved.

I was looking out at the ocean when I heard footsteps behind me. "All set?" I asked when I turned around and saw Luisa and her mother.

"Yes," Luisa responded. "I'd like to leave as soon as possible."

Sera walked out of the kitchen, and I was happy to see both she and Press were smiling.

"I'll grab your bags," I said at the same time Press offered to.

"We'll both get them," he said, going ahead of me.

When Sera followed, I realized she would have a bag too. "All good?" I asked.

"He apologized."

"I was hoping he would."

"I understand, though. He was protecting you."

"There are times people need to be given the benefit of the doubt." I was talking as much about her mom and my dad as I was about Press.

While I wanted to get the conversation we needed to have over with, I didn't want to have it over the phone. As much as I wished it weren't necessary, I was relieved when he insisted my mom and him cut their trip short. As Tryst had said, whatever had happened was big enough that it stood between Sera and me. Once everything was out in the open, I planned to confess my feelings for her and hoped she felt the same.

Press made it obvious he wanted to come along, but it wasn't necessary to take two cars, so he'd be following us needlessly.

"I'll see to it Sorcha invites you to dinner," I offered.

"Tonight?"

"I'll see what I can do."

The drive from Seahorse to Butler Ranch took a little over thirty minutes. When we pulled up to the main house, Jada Yáñez and her mother were sitting on the front porch, talking with Doc's parents.

"Sorcha, give the girl a moment to breathe," Laird called after his wife when she rushed down the steps and over to the SUV.

"You could be more hospitable," she shouted over her shoulder at him. "Come and get their bags, for goodness' sake."

"It's okay, Mrs. Butler. If you tell me where they should go, I can manage," I said.

"It's Sorcha, Noah Ridge, and my Laird can help."

I figured there wasn't much point in arguing with her, especially after Laird took Luisa's bag and motioned with his head for me to follow with her mother's.

"Best to let Sorcha get everyone feeling comfortable," he said when we got to the first of two Scottish-style stone cottages, both two-storied replications of the main house. "Sorcha and I are right next door, if the ladies need anything," he added.

"Oh, I thought Naughton lived in one of these."

"He did, but when he married and the baby was born, my wife insisted they move into the main house. She says it's less upkeep for her in the smaller one, but I know what she was really after was for Naughton and Bradley to stay on here and raise their family."

"They have one child, right?"

"Aye. A boy they call Charlie. But another's on the way."

"Congratulations. That's wonderful news."

"Mark my words, soon your mother and father will start pestering you to give them grandchildren."

"No doubt." I chuckled and followed him inside.

There was a time, not long ago, when those words would've felt like a knife to my heart. Now, instead of thinking about Alex and Maddox, Sera was the first person who came to mind, and I wondered if she wished to have a family. It was one of so many things I had to talk to her about. However, until I was sure she wanted this attraction between us to turn into more, I'd curb my enthusiasm.

"There are three bedrooms on the second floor. We'll put all the bags in the largest and let the ladies decide who will stay where. When they do, you can move them."

I smiled and nodded.

By the time we returned to the porch, Sorcha and her daughter-in-law Bradley had brought two platters of food.

"Can I help with anything?" I asked.

"Aye," Sorcha answered. "You and Laird can get the rest."

I followed the grumbling man into the house, where there were two more platters plus one tray holding plates, napkins, and utensils and another with a pitcher of lemonade and glasses.

"There'll be no going hungry if my wife has anything to say about it."

"You're both very generous."

"Aye, well, your parents would do the same. How are they, by the way?"

"They've been traveling, but will be back tomorrow."

"See to it Sorcha knows. She'll be sure to invite them to dinner."

Yet another reason why we needed to have our conversation as soon as possible.

"This was such a good idea. Thank you," Sera said when I asked her to take a walk with me. "Especially inviting Jada over."

"I'm glad it worked out. While I know Press would've preferred your sister remain at Seahorse, Sorcha Butler will make all three of you feel at home here."

She studied me.

"What?" I asked.

"Why do you think Press would prefer Luisa remain at Seahorse?"

"Uh, I guess he's being a bit of a mother hen."

"Not the way I ever would've described Press," she said, laughing.

34

Seraphina

"It is so beautiful here," I said when we crested a rise and a view of the rolling hills of Paso Robles all the way to the Pacific Ocean opened up.

"I've only been on the ranch a few times, for events, but it is definitely one of the best pieces of property in the area."

While what he'd said was innocuous enough, his voice was tinged with tension.

"Noah, is something wrong?"

"Mind if we sit?" he asked, pointing to a bench on the edge of a vineyard.

"You're worrying me," I said when he took my hand in his.

"I feel almost like a teenager saying this, but I really like you, Sera. More, if I'm honest."

"If we're being honest, I feel the same way. But…"

"There's more we need to talk about."

I nodded. "I know there is." While we'd found my sister and had a general plan of action where William

Cooley was concerned, there was still the issue of what had happened between our parents.

"When Tryst came by my place the other day to tell me what he'd learned about Cooley, he pressed me to call my dad. He and my mom are on their way back from Australia now."

"Oh. So, um, what did he say?"

"Only that I wasn't imagining I wasn't your mother's favorite person. He admitted something had happened but didn't want to talk about it over the phone."

"Can I tell you what my mom told me?" I asked.

"It's completely up to you. If you'd rather wait, I understand."

"I don't." I told him she'd accused Hewitt Ridge of stealing my father's wine formulas, specifically for Vineyard Twenty-Seven.

"My father was in a coma from that night until he died. He never woke up from it, so I don't know how she'd know. However, she seems adamant."

Noah cocked his head. "Back to being honest. I can't see my father doing what your mom accused him of. It wouldn't be like him. I'm not saying it didn't happen, because my dad admitted something did, but stealing formulas? It would be completely out of character for the man I believe he is."

"I don't disagree. I remember my mother saying the deal your dad made with mine when he bought the estate was generous. What would've made her change her mind and accuse him of stealing something?"

He looked out at the ocean. "I wish I knew, but I guess, soon, we both will."

"Tryst told me he saw my mom and your dad together. Before you have the same reaction I did, he doesn't think they were having an affair. He thought she might have gone to him for help. Sorry if I worried you for a sec."

"My dad worships the ground my mom walks on and vice versa. So, yeah, if he'd had an affair, it would have made me question everything about my life."

"I want you to know I checked, and my father never filed any patents. None. The other thing that doesn't make sense to me is, *if* your dad used his formula for the wine made from that vineyard, why is it so good when what my dad experimented with put us into bankruptcy?"

"I gotta tell you, as much as I'm dreading this conversation, I'll be happy when it's behind us."

I rested my head on his shoulder. "Me too, Noah."

By the time Noah went back to Seahorse with Press so he could leave his car with me, and my sister, mom, and I went to bed, my belly was full from the wonderful meal Sorcha had served and I was exhausted. While I hoped that meant I'd sleep, I doubted I would.

I couldn't decide whether to tell my mother Noah's parents would be coming to Butler Ranch tomorrow. Or at least his dad would be. Part of me didn't want to ambush her, but another part was afraid she'd refuse to talk to Hewitt, Noah and me. Until we could get everyone in one room and talk this out, it would forever hang over our heads.

As I'd anticipated, I tossed and turned to the point where Luisa asked if I'd sleep in another room. She and I had decided to stay in the room with two twin beds and offered my mom the biggest of the three.

When I closed the door of the bedroom behind me and walked a little way down the hall, I saw the larger bedroom's door was wide open. I peeked into the other room and saw my mom asleep in it.

Knowing I'd be up for a while, I crept downstairs, pulled out my laptop, then put it back. If I started it up, I'd check my email. If there was anything from Cooley or anyone else in the DA's office, it would only make it harder for me to get any rest.

I went into the kitchen, not because I was hungry, since I couldn't eat another bite, but in search of something that might help me wind down. I found a box of chamomile tea bags in the cupboard and filled the kettle sitting on the stove with water. I'd poured the boiling water over a tea bag at the same time my mom walked in.

"Looks like we had the same idea," she said.

"Want a cup? No caffeine."

"Thanks, baby," she said when I set the cup in front of her and filled another for myself. "Can't sleep?" she asked.

I sighed. "No. Too much on my mind."

"Me too."

"Something with Luisa?" I asked.

She put her hand on top of mine. "No, not with your sister. You really care about Noah Ridge, don't you?"

"It's more than that. I'm in love with him."

"I can tell. You look at him the same way I used to look at your father."

"Tell me what really happened with Hewitt, Mom. I'm sorry, but I don't believe he stole Dad's formulas."

Her eyes filled with tears, and she turned away, but she didn't get up and walk out. She took a deep breath and let it out slowly. "Your dad and I had a terrible fight the night of the accident. He found out I'd gone to Hewitt and asked for help when the winery was going under. It was the reason he'd made the offer to buy it. Your father was absolutely furious with me for going behind his back."

"What else happened?"

"He stormed into the bedroom, and I heard him on the phone, talking to Hewitt, demanding they meet. When he came out, he had a manila envelope in his hand. It contained his formulas. I'm sure of it."

"What makes you think Noah's father stole them?"

"They weren't in the car when the police went through it. I asked them to go back and check."

"You're *sure* that's what he took with him?"

"Almost positive."

"What do you think Dad planned to do with them?"

"Your father was a very prideful man, Seraphina. While I don't know for certain, my guess is his intention was to give them to Hewitt in exchange for helping us. It was really the only thing of value he had left. Other than the house, which we ended up losing anyway."

"If he gave them to Hewitt, you can't accuse the man of stealing them, Mom."

"But how could he take them? How has he been able to live with himself, making so much money off something your father created? And there we were, destitute."

"Did you confront him about it?"

"I thought about it, but with your father in the hospital and the deaths of that family, it was all I could do to get out of bed every day. If it weren't for you girls, I don't know I would have."

"But it's been eating away at you all these years."

"It's the only thing that makes sense, Seraphina."

"It's one explanation, Mom. If what you think did happen and Dad gave them to him, you don't know Hewitt ever used them. There's no way to prove he did. I looked. There are no patents. I told you that before."

"Why wouldn't he give them back? At least then, you girls would have something of your father's. It doesn't matter if they're worthless. They were a piece of him."

"There's something I have to tell you."

My mom took several deep breaths. "What?"

"Hewitt Ridge will be here tomorrow. Noah contacted him and asked what happened. His father wouldn't tell him over the phone, but he said something did. He and Noah's mom are returning from Australia tonight."

When she tried to stand, I held onto her arm.

"I didn't tell you, because I was afraid you'd refuse to meet with him. We have to, Mom. We have to know the real story so we can move on with our lives. All of us."

She shook her head.

"Do it for me, Mom. I want to spend my life with Noah, and while I don't know for sure he wants the same thing, I want us to have a fighting chance. He's a good man. Look what he did for us, for Luisa."

"I'll think about it. I can't promise I'll be able to go through with it. I've spent so many years believing he took advantage of us while I had to work my fingers to the bone to pay the rent on my crappy apartment.

Thank God you and your sister were able to get scholarships and go to college."

"I understand you'd feel resentful. Honestly, I do. But all this anger you have inside may be directed toward a man who doesn't deserve it."

I called Noah the next morning and told him about the conversation my mom and I had had the night before. "She's still asleep. I don't know if she'll agree to talk to your father, but at least now, I have a better idea of what she believes happened."

"Would you prefer it if I talk to my father alone?" he asked.

"I thought about it. I mean, I haven't slept at all. But, no. I need to be there. I hope you understand."

"Of course I do."

"I just hope my mom will be there too."

As much as I wanted to see Noah earlier in the day, before he arrived at Butler Ranch with his father, we agreed it would be best if we waited. He said his parents' flight would land at eleven, and as long as it wasn't delayed, they'd arrive at the ranch at one.

My sister and I were sitting in the kitchen when my mom came downstairs at half after noon.

"Hey, Mom. I made lunch. Want to join us?"

"I'm not hungry, baby."

I stood and pulled out a chair. "Will you at least sit with us?"

She shook her head. "I'm going for a walk."

"Noah and his dad will be here in less than a half hour. I hope you'll be with us to hear what he has to say."

My mom cupped my cheek. "I can't, Seraphina. You hear him out. If you believe him, I'll eventually learn to accept it."

I was on the verge of bursting into tears. *Eventually?* So if I believed Hewitt didn't do anything wrong, a wedge would still remain between my mother and Noah's family?

"Mom, I'm begging you. Please. Do it for me. I know it will be hard, but *please*."

When my mother left the room, I didn't have it in me to follow. I sank into the chair, put my head in my hands, and cried.

"Seraphina? Do you want to tell me what's going on?" Luisa asked in a voice barely above a whisper.

It took me several minutes before I could speak, but when I'd finally stopped crying, I told her everything I knew.

When I finished, Luisa got up from the table. "Why didn't she ever say anything?"

"Maybe she didn't think there was any reason to. Not until Noah Ridge showed up to help us find you."

"Hewitt Ridge doesn't have Dad's formulas."

"What do you mean?"

"I do. I've had them since before the accident."

I was stunned. Almost too much to speak. "What are you talking about?"

"As young as I was, I still knew what was going on. I knew Dad was drinking way too much. One night, Mom made me go in and say goodnight to him. He was sitting at his desk, staring at all these papers, and crying. I almost left, but he called my name, so I went over to him."

"Then what happened?"

"He turned his chair so I could sit on his knee. I asked what he was doing, and he pointed to all of it. He said it was his life's work and it was all worthless. He said he was worthless. He started to ball them all up and throw them away, but I begged him not to. I told him to give them to me." Luisa smiled.

"What?"

"You know I was named for his mother?"

"Yeah?"

"He said I sounded exactly like her, so he gave them to me."

I didn't need to look at my watch to know that unless she had them with her, which I knew she didn't, I wouldn't have enough time to go and get them before Noah and his dad arrived. "Where are they?"

"In the old cigar box."

"What old cigar box?"

"I think it's on one of the shelves in the living room."

I grabbed her wrist. "How come Mom never knew? She never opened it? You never thought to tell her you had them?"

When Luisa pulled away from me, I realized I was frightening her.

"I'm sorry. You didn't know. How could you? I didn't."

"It has an insert. I put them underneath it."

"Okay. Good. At least we know where they are."

It dawned on me that if this wasn't about the formulas, what reason did Hewitt Ridge have to want to talk to Noah, my mom, and me in person? What the hell else had happened?

I was on my way out the door to look for my mom when Noah and Hewitt drove up.

"I'll see if I can find her," Luisa offered.

"Are you sure?"

"How far could she have gotten? She left less than fifteen minutes ago."

"Hi," I said when Noah got out of the car. "Sorry, um, my mom went for a walk and hasn't come back yet."

"It's okay. We can wait." Noah reached out and held my hand.

His father walked over to us.

"Dad, this is Seraphina Reeve. Sera, meet my father."

"It's a pleasure," he said. "And I want you to know how sorry I am about all this."

I looked from him to his son. "I'm the one who's sorry. I found out *we* have the formulas. Luisa had them all this time."

"Formulas?" Hewitt asked.

"My mom thought that's why you and my dad met. She thought he gave them to you."

"I'm lost."

"Sera's mom thought you stole her father's wine formulas, Dad."

He seemed genuinely confused. "I don't know anything about them."

"Do you want to come inside?"

"Sure, but uh, what about your mom and sister?" Noah asked.

I looked over my shoulder as if they'd magically appear. "I'm not sure."

"I'll go look for them," he offered.

Not knowing what else to do, I took him up on it.

"Maybe I should go with Noah and help look for them," Hewitt offered.

"I don't think that's a good idea. Look, I know none of this is your fault, but before my mom left, she told me she didn't want to meet with us."

"Understood. I don't want to make her more uncomfortable than she already is."

"I don't know about you, but I could really use a glass of wine."

"I'll join you."

Hewitt followed me into the kitchen.

"Sorry," I said, motioning to the mess on the table. "We were finishing lunch."

"You pick out the wine, and I'll clean this up. If you're done."

"Yep," I said, smiling since there was no food left on the plates.

Hewitt stacked the dishes and carried them to the sink.

"Thanks, I can take it from here. Is this one okay?" I handed him a bottle of Butler Ranch Chardonnay and an opener. "Glasses are in there." I pointed to a cabinet.

"Perfect."

I rinsed the dishes and shoved them into the dishwasher, knowing if I didn't, Hewitt would probably insist on doing it himself.

"Shall we sit in here?" he asked when I wiped my hands on a towel.

"Sure."

He pulled out my chair and sat after I did.

"I'm so sorry about this. It's all a misunderstanding that could have been cleared up if my mom, my sister, and I had simply talked about it."

"I'm not sure what you're referring to with the formulas, but I would like to tell you what happened that night."

"Maybe we should wait."

The door opened at the same time I finished my sentence, and my mom, Luisa, and Noah rushed inside. "We were almost drenched," said Luisa.

Noah's father stood. "Hello, Leah."

"Hewitt."

"This must be Luisa." He stepped forward and shook her hand. "It's nice to meet you."

"You too," said my sister, motioning me to join her in the living room.

"Excuse me," I muttered.

"I didn't get a chance to tell mom anything except that I knew where the formulas were. Then it started to rain, and Noah found us."

I nodded. "At least she knows that much."

When we returned to the kitchen, Hewitt had opened another bottle and poured three more drinks. "This was Seraphina's idea, and I think it's a good one." He held up a glass, and my mother took it. Luisa did the same.

"Should we go into the other room?" I asked. "Or should we stay here?" God, I was so nervous I was shaking.

Noah walked around the table and pulled out a chair. "Let's stay here, Sera." When I sat, he took the seat next to me, then held my hand. After my mom and Luisa sat down, Hewitt did too.

"Can I start?" Luisa asked.

"Go ahead," I told her.

"I don't know exactly what this is about, but Seraphina mentioned our mom thought you had my father's wine formulas." She turned to Hewitt, then to my mom. "I'm sorry. I didn't realize you were looking for them. They're at the apartment."

"That's what you said, but I don't understand why you had them."

"May I continue?" Luisa asked.

When my mother nodded, my sister reiterated the story she'd told me. Our mom's eyes were wide, and by the time Luisa finished, I knew she'd realized her mistake.

"I'm sorry," she said, looking directly at Hewitt. "I accused you of something unfairly. My husband had an envelope with him the night of the accident, and

I overheard him demand you meet him. I assumed… And then, when nothing was found in the car…" My mother put her head in her hands.

"Leah, I know what was in the envelope," said Noah's father.

She moved her hands from her face and looked at him.

"It was the contract for the sale of the vineyards and winery. He wanted to get out of it, but I told him it was too late. The deal had been wrapped up two weeks earlier. The bank had been paid off, and the title company was finalizing the deed."

"What happened to the contract?" I asked. "My mom sent the police to check the car, and they didn't find it."

"He took out a lighter and set it on fire." Hewitt took a deep breath and looked down at his hands. "I walked out." When he looked up at my mother, he had tears in his eyes.

"I've never forgiven myself for that night. I knew Joseph was drinking. I should've stayed." Tears spilled over onto his cheeks. "Instead, I turned my back on him and left. I'm sorry."

"Dad," said Noah, putting his hand on his father's shoulder.

Hewitt covered his face and shook his head. He took another deep breath, then lowered his hands. "I know there's no way to make it up to you—"

"It isn't your fault, Hewitt," my mother said, and I gripped her hand as she stared into Noah's father's eyes. "It isn't your fault," she repeated.

Hewitt turned to Noah. "I'm sorry, son."

"Don't apologize, Dad. Not to me."

He shook his head. "It's my greatest source of shame."

"I knew he'd been drinking. I'm the one who should've stopped him," said my mom.

"I knew too. We all knew. And as much as we wish we could go back and change the events of that night, we can't. My dad is the one who got behind the wheel of that car and drove to the bar in the first place. He shouldn't have left the house. We shouldn't have let him. Whoever sold him liquor, shouldn't have." I looked up at Noah's father. "You weren't the only person there the night it happened who could've stepped in and helped him. We all have regrets." I got up and walked out.

While every other person at the table had tears in their eyes or was crying, I knew I was about to break down. I had to get out of the room. I would've left the house if Noah hadn't stopped me.

"Shh," he soothed, stroking my hair with one hand while he held me close to him with the other. "Come with me." When I didn't move, he lifted me in his arms and carried me up the stairs.

"Which one is yours?" he asked.

"None of them. I slept in the same room with Luisa." I pointed to the largest of the rooms. "That one is empty, though."

After carrying me in, Noah gently set me on the bed, then rested beside me.

"I left everyone sitting there," I said, trying to get up.

"They'll be fine. You, on the other hand, are dead on your feet."

"I feel like I've gone through the wringer and was hung out to dry."

He smiled. "Close your eyes."

"I can't. I have to—"

Noah kissed me. "You have to rest."

35

Ridge

Part of me felt as though I should go downstairs, but as soon as Sera fell asleep, there was no way I'd risk waking her. It felt too good holding her in my arms.

Everything that happened the night of the accident was tragic, but as she'd said, no one person was at fault. Her dad had driven drunk, and again as she'd said, it began there. There were several points along the way when something could have prevented the accident and the horrific outcome. But nothing had.

Now, we all needed to heal. My dad, Leah, Luisa, Sera, and me. One place came to mind—*El Lugar de Curación*—Tryst's ranch in Mexico. While the timing might not be right, eventually, I wanted Sera and me to return there and experience it under different circumstances than when her sister was missing.

The following week, several things happened. First, Sera arranged for the two of us to meet the woman who'd held the position of ADA before her. Now, she was a senior investigator with the Internal Affairs Division of the Fourth Judicial District Attorney's Office. She'd pursued the position with a specific target in mind—William Cooley—and had spent the last few months compiling evidence against him.

Adding Sera's experiences of being blackmailed, having her apartment bugged, as well as the proof she'd compiled of the illegalities surrounding the Los Caballeros investigation, made the internal affairs case much stronger.

Sera and I were equally stunned when we heard from her two days later that an indictment would be handed down within the coming week. Coincidentally, there were thirty-three counts against Cooley, the same number his father had been charged with.

At first, Sera had requested a leave of absence from the DA's office, but after learning about the impending indictment, she'd turned in her resignation instead.

"I can't devote the kind of time and energy a position like interim DA requires. Luisa comes first," she'd said.

"I might know of another position opening up. One with more flexibility." I winked.

"What?"

"Ridge Winery's legal counsel is getting ready to retire and close up shop. I know my father wants to hire a new attorney since he asked me if you'd be interested in the job."

"I'm a prosecutor."

"I'll let him know—"

"Wait. I'd be willing to discuss it at least."

The following day, Sera, my parents, Dalton, and I met, and when the meeting ended, she was on retainer.

A full week had passed since Sera, her sister, and her mom came to stay at Butler Ranch. Press spent the better part of every day visiting Luisa, and I spent every minute I could with Sera.

On our hour drive from San Luis Obispo to Butler Ranch after our second and last meeting with the internal affairs investigator, I convinced her to stop at my place on See Canyon Road. I'd used the excuse of wanting to check on the progress being made on the house, but what I really wanted was time alone with her. I knew she was on to me when she suggested we stop by Soto's on our way and have a picnic like we'd had before.

"I can't believe it's over," she said as we sat out on the deck, finishing our wine. "Luisa is safe, my mom knows your dad didn't steal my father's wine formulas, and Cooley is headed to prison, where he belongs." Her expression changed. "It isn't over with the human traffickers, though. Have you received any kind of update about what happened after we left England?"

"According to Doc Butler, their firm is leading the ongoing investigation. It may be months or longer before we know the final outcome. One thing we learned from what happened with Luisa is the ring is far bigger than initially thought."

"What about Jorge? I guess that wasn't his name."

"While Manual Varilla attempted to negotiate protection in exchange for telling us Luisa was on that ship, his role as an informant is far from over."

"I don't know how to begin thanking you for all you've done for my family," she said, staring out at the ocean.

"It wasn't only me."

Sera smiled. "Some of it was. Especially getting me a new job. I make more on retainer for Ridge than I made working at the DA's office. So far, it doesn't seem like there will be much for me to do."

"I have one idea."

She studied me. "Go ahead."

"I'd like to experiment with your father's formulas. First, though, you'd need to file patents for them on behalf of your family as well as negotiate a fee for their use."

She cocked her head. "You know as well as I do they were failures."

"I'm not so sure, which is why I want to try a couple out and see what I can do with them."

"They all require grapes now used in the Vineyard Twenty-Seven Blend."

"Maybe the new wine will be better."

She raised a brow. "You arranged for me to work for your family's business. Now you're making sure my mother has an income stream. I sense you'll ensure it whether you actually use the formulas or not. What's next? Are you planning to give Luisa a job too?"

"She is close to graduating summa cum laude with an MBA. Who wouldn't consider her an asset to their organization?"

"Noah…I appreciate all of it, but it's too much."

I took the glass from her hand and set it, along with mine, on the table where we'd shared our picnic dinner.

I wrapped her in my arms and stared into her eyes. "It could never be enough for me to show you what you mean to me."

Her gaze stayed riveted to mine.

"I love you, Seraphina Reeve."

"I love you, Noah Ridge."

While I'd told myself I'd been in love with Alex Avila, now I knew I never was. It was as though once my heart was released from the ties I'd kept around it for so long, I could finally experience *real love*. I'd never felt freer or happier.

When we kissed, it wasn't simply sharing that love; it signified everything standing between us falling away. What remained were two people who'd started out believing we were adversaries, realizing instead we were soulmates.

"The day you and I first stood on this deck together, I had a fantasy."

"So did I."

"Tell me what it was, Sera."

She shook her head. "You go first."

"Better if I show you."

One by one, I unfastened the buttons on her shirt, then eased it off her shoulders. I reached behind and unhooked her bra.

She wove her fingers in my hair when I knelt in front of her. "I like your fantasy."

"It doesn't bother you that we're out in the open?"

"It isn't like anyone can see us from here, Noah. And even if they could, I don't think I could bring myself to care."

"Let's get these off," I said, leaning down to remove her shoes. I unfastened her jeans and pulled them along with her panties over the curve of her lush ass and down her legs.

I drank in the sight of Sera standing naked before me, the sunset's glow bathing her in warm, soft light. She was so beautiful, so perfect. It was hard for me to tear my eyes away. My mouth, though, was too eager for a taste.

"Tell me what you want, Sera," I said before my lips found the tip of her breast. I blew cool air on it, then circled it with my tongue before capturing it with my teeth. "More of that?" I asked when her hands pulled at my hair.

"Yes, God, more," she pleaded.

In the same way I'd pictured it, I ran my tongue down past her belly button. Then spread her legs, licking up and down, exploring her with my mouth. The sounds of her pleasure mixed with the crashing waves of the ocean far beneath us. When I gently sucked her clit, Seraphina's cries echoed through See Canyon.

I felt her legs giving out, gathered her in my arms, and carried her over to the daybed.

"Lie still and watch," I said when she reached out for me. I pulled my shirt over my head, then unfastened my belt and jeans, letting them fall to the floor after I'd toed off my shoes.

Her heated gaze ran the length of me, and my already stiff cock grew steel-like. She licked her lips and put her hand between her spread legs.

"That's mine now, Sera."

She smiled but didn't move her fingers away from her glistening pussy. I grabbed her ankles, pulled her to the edge of the round cushion, and held both her wrists with one hand.

"Mine," I repeated, inserting two fingers into her wetness, curling them until her body spasmed and her back arched. I replaced my fingers with my cock, thrusting deep inside her, wanting to be part of the orgasm she was in the midst of.

"I love you," I said when her eyes met mine. I slowly moved inside her, bringing my cock to the edge of her pussy, then thrusting deeply again and again. All the while, her eyes remained riveted to mine.

I dug my fingers into the flesh of her ass, grinding into her, feeling myself on the precipice, but there was one thing I was waiting for before I let myself go.

My eyes begged her to say the words I needed to hear, and she did. "I love you, Noah."

My body jolted in ecstasy, but I couldn't look away. I wanted her to see what being with her did to me. When she cried out, her fingers digging into my arms, I finally gave into the release, experiencing greater pleasure than I knew existed.

I held myself above her, my arms shaking and my cock twitching in her still-spasming pussy. Finally, I eased from her warmth and lay my body next to hers.

Sera turned to her side and put her hand on my heart. Neither of us spoke, but we didn't need to. We'd already said the most important words there were. I let myself drift into a peaceful sleep when I heard her breathing even out.

When I woke, the sun was gone and the moon was high in the sky. I got the blanket out of the ottoman and put it over both our bodies.

"Noah?" I heard her moan as her hands reached for me.

"I'm here."

"I need more," she mewled as she kissed her way down my body like I had hers.

We'd reached out for each other throughout the night, our bodies joined until the glow of the sunrise in the east blanketed the deck in the same warm light the sunset had the night before. I knew Sera was awake too when I felt her fingers trailing down my chest. I grabbed her wrist, and she looked up at me.

"What's wrong?" she asked.

"Absolutely nothing." I leaned forward and kissed her, then pulled back, staring into her eyes like I had each time we made love. "Marry me, Seraphina."

"If you're asking, my answer is yes."

I kissed her again. Harder and deeper. All the love I felt for her pouring out of me.

When we finally rolled off the daybed, it was close to ten.

"You seriously need a kitchen. Or at least a coffee-maker," she grumbled. "And a shower."

"I've got one of those covered." I took her hand and pulled her out to the deck and around the corner to where I'd installed an outdoor shower.

"I hope you never get neighbors," she said as we lathered each other's naked bodies out in the open with a view of the canyon.

"*We* won't."

36

"Everything okay?" Noah asked after I ended my call with Luisa.

"It's all good. Press is there, and they're having a late breakfast with my mom."

"Speaking of breakfast. Do we have time to go to Huck's?"

"If you hadn't suggested it, I would have."

When we arrived, there was one open table left. It was the same one we'd sat at the first morning when I threatened Brix and Los Caballeros and he'd walked out.

Like the time in between when we were here, Noah slid beside me onto the bench seat and leaned over to kiss my forehead.

"Two Cajun omelets today, or are you lovebirds mixing it up?" asked Barb when she brought two cups of coffee to the table without our asking.

"Works for me," I said.

"Me too," Noah added.

"You shoulda ordered pancakes, kids, cuz your syrupy sweetness is overflowing," she said as she walked away.

"I can't help it. I'm deliriously happy."

"So am I." Noah leaned over to kiss me again, this time on the lips.

"Hey, Mad-man, look who's here."

When I opened my eyes, I saw Alex and her husband, Maddox. walking toward us. He was carrying their baby. Alex slid onto the bench seat across from us, and Maddox pulled up a chair.

"Mornin'," he said, holding out one hand to shake Ridge's. I waved, and both he and the baby waved back.

"So, how goes it?" Alex asked, wiggling her eyebrows.

I laughed. "It goes pretty great."

"Seems like it. I'm really happy for you both," she said, looking first at Noah, then at me.

"I asked Sera to marry me," he blurted.

"And?"

"I said yes."

Alex clapped her hands and reached out for Coco. "I'd say mimosas are in order, wouldn't you?"

"I sure would," said Maddox, standing and motioning to Barb, who moments later, brought five glasses, a carafe of orange juice, and a bottle of sparkling wine.

"Thanks, but I don't think she's old enough to join us yet," said Alex, bouncing the baby on her knee.

Barb picked up a glass, poured it half full with wine, then added the OJ. She brought the glass to her lips and guzzled the whole thing. "Cheers!" she said, walking away and taking the glass with her.

When we drove through the ranch gates and past the main house, Luisa and my mom were sitting on the bench outside the cottage's front door.

"Hey," I said, walking over and kissing my sister's cheek after we got out of the car. "Where's Press?"

"He had to go. Something about being summoned to spend the afternoon with his mother."

"Speaking of being summoned, I'm supposed to help Sorcha and Bradley with tonight's dinner," said my mom, standing and kissing my cheek like I had Luisa's. When she walked away, I took her seat on the bench.

"I should probably go check in with my parents," said Noah, stuffing his hands in his pockets.

Luisa looked up at him. "Before you do, there's something I want to talk to you both about."

"Go ahead," I said when Noah pulled a chair over from in front of the cottage.

"There are two things. First, finishing my degree. Press said he thought my professors might let me do the last few assignments and exams independently, given the reason I was gone."

"I'm sure they would." I looked over at Noah, who nodded.

"What was the other thing?" I asked.

Luisa looked from me to Noah. "Press said his uncle or your uncle or someone's uncle owns a ranch in Mexico."

I put my hand on hers and squeezed. "We stayed there when we were first looking for you."

"The man who owns it is Brix Avila's uncle," Noah clarified.

"Press also said it's *magical*."

I smiled. "He did?"

"Mom said the same thing about it."

I was surprised she had. "So, what about it?"

"Press said he could take us there in his plane if we wanted to go."

"Press has been a busy guy," Noah said under his breath. I looked over at him and smiled.

Luisa squeezed my fingers like I had hers. "I want to go, and I know you'll have a fit unless you go too. Then, when we get back, I'll finish out my classes."

"Have you brought this up to Mom?"

"I asked her about the ranch, but not about visiting. I figured you'd be the harder one to convince."

When Noah laughed, I reached over and smacked his leg. "Hush, you."

Luisa pulled a phone out I hadn't realized she had. "Hang on. It's Press. Be right back." She went inside the house.

"What do you think about this thing with my sister and Press?" I whispered.

"This thing? Do you think it's a thing?"

"Did you hear how many times she said his name? Press said this. Press said that. Press hung the moon."

He chuckled. "He has been spending a lot of time with her."

"Why?"

"I think he feels a certain responsibility for your sister. He was there when she was rescued. He and I talked about it once and agreed his protective instincts were on overdrive. Does it bother you?"

"Not really, but…I'm worried she's going to get attached to him. Then his girlfriend will fly in from Australia like Beau's."

Noah shook his head. "I assure you, Press does not have a girlfriend."

"Not really the point, my love."

He got up from the chair and sat beside me. "You wanna know what I think?"

"I do."

"I think it would be the perfect place for a wedding."

Epilogue

Ridge

"There's no better place on earth to get married," said Brix. "I speak from experience." He patted my shoulders. "How're you feeling?"

"Honestly? Great."

"No cold feet?" my brother asked.

"That doesn't happen when you're marrying the right woman," Brix told Dalton.

He was right. I was anxious, sure, but only because I couldn't wait for Sera to be my wife, and I agreed. There was nowhere better in the world for me to become her husband.

We'd delayed our trip to Mexico for six weeks for a few reasons. One, to plan the wedding. Next, at the same time Luisa finished her degree, which Sera talked her into doing first, she filed the patents on her father's wine formulas and negotiated a contract for our use of them. Leah's only protest in the process was to say she thought we were paying too much money.

Tryst, who had become an ordained minister before Brix and Addy's wedding, offered to perform the ceremony, which would be starting in less than fifteen minutes.

"We gotta go," I said after realizing what time it was.

"We're a two-minute walk away," said Zin, handing me a glass of water. "Figured you'd want to wait until after the wedding to start drinking wine."

"How are Luisa and Leah doing?" I asked Press.

"The only person who will look more beautiful today than they do is Seraphina. Your mum too, of course," he added when I raised a brow.

I finished the glass of water, straightened my sleeves, and made sure my boutonniere was on securely. "I'm ready."

"Come on, mates," said Beau, opening the door of the *casita*. My dearest friends, men who were all like brothers to me, whom I sat beside at Los Caballeros' table, walked together to the temple, where we saw Tryst waiting at the front door. Alex stood with him. When we got close, she walked toward me.

"I'm happy for you, Ridge," she said. "You and Seraphina will build a wonderful life together, just like Maddox and I have."

"I need to thank you."

"Okay. Why'd you say it like that?"

"Because if you hadn't dumped me and married Maddox, I never would've opened my heart to the woman I was really meant to be with."

"My pleasure," she said, winking. "Come on. Time for me to give away the groom."

Keep reading for a
preview of the next book in the
Wicked Winemakers Central Coast
First Label Series,
Press' Passion

His life was structured by obligations.
Her days were haunted by survival.
Together, they discover healing requires
more than time.

LAVERY

I've always put duty before desire, until Luisa Reeve awakened feelings I can't ignore. When danger threatens her life, I'll stop at nothing to keep her safe, even as an unexpected death in my family pulls me in another direction. As my heart opens to her strength and vulnerability, I'm caught between new love and old responsibilities. Can I find a way to be there for those who need me without losing the woman who breathed new purpose into my existence?

LUISA

After surviving a kidnapping by human traffickers, I'm fighting to rebuild myself piece by piece. When

Press Barrett entered my life with his quiet strength, I never expected he would become my sanctuary. I regain sleep when he's nearby, yet wonder if I'm substituting one dependency for another. Is the safety I feel with him genuine, or is my trauma clouding my ability to recognize when I'm becoming vulnerable in unhealthy ways?

1

Press

I shifted slightly and peeked at the other side of the altar at Luisa Reeve, the most beautiful creature God had been so kind to grace the rest of us lowly beings with. We both stood to bear witness to the union between her sister, Seraphina, and one of my closest friends, Noah Ridge. While I wasn't the best man—an honor reserved for Ridge's best mate, Brix—I was the first groomsman. Thus, allowing me to look unnoticed.

The woman was a recent victim of a human trafficking ring, abducted by a man she'd believed was her loving boyfriend, yet she wore her bravery like a badge.

In the days immediately following her rescue, I'd invited Luisa and her mother to stay at the estate I'd lovingly named Seahorse, located just south of Cambria, on the Central Coast of California. She was safer there than she would've been at her mother's apartment in San Luis Obispo, where there was little to no security.

Seahorse, on the other hand, had been outfitted with the most advanced technology in existence. No one could enter the gates off Pacific Coast Highway without both retinal and palm scans. Same with every entrance to the main house.

While she was there, I'd witnessed her transformation from a victim to a survivor and, with it, had a front-row seat to the wonder of the woman. She was extraordinarily intelligent, her beauty had no equal even among the world's most recognizable supermodels, and her heart, well, it was soft and kind, gentle and loving. The evil bastards who had taken her and transported her across the ocean hadn't broken the spirit of the woman who stood behind her sister, tear-filled eyes smiling and proud.

To say I loved Luisa would be unimaginable to some, and yet I did with all my being. When she raised her head and gazed in my direction, my heart first leaped, then fell when her eyes looked beyond me to my brother, who stood behind me. The man she was in love with rather than me.

Keep reading for a sneak peek at
the first book in the
K19 Allied Intelligence Team One Series—
Code Name: Ares

**He's a disgraced CIA operative seeking redemption.
She's a brilliant MI5 agent who
won't risk her heart again.
Together, they'll hunt the world's
most dangerous traffickers—
and discover a love worth fighting for.**

PHILIP

As a former CIA operative, I thought I'd seen it all. Then I met her—Margeaux "Nemesis" Jordan, the brilliant and infuriatingly stubborn leader of the UK's anti-trafficking task force. Now, we're forced to work together, leading a UN coalition against a global human trafficking network. It should be simple: focus on the mission, ignore the attraction. But with every lead we chase, every life we save, I find myself falling harder. In a world of shadows and danger, can I protect both the innocent and my heart? Or will choosing duty mean losing the one woman who could be my perfect match?

MARGEAUX

As a former CIA operative, I thought I'd seen it all. Then I met her—Margeaux "Nemesis" Jordan, the brilliant and infuriatingly stubborn leader of the UK's anti-trafficking task force. Now, we're forced to work together, leading a UN coalition against a global human trafficking network. It should be simple: focus on the mission, ignore the attraction. But with every lead we chase, every life we save, I find myself falling harder. In a world of shadows and danger, can I protect both the innocent and my heart? Or will choosing duty mean losing the one woman who could be my perfect match?

1

Ares

"He's ridiculous. I mean, have you seen him? He's a walking, talking cover model for a romance book," I overheard MI5's human trafficking expert say as I approached the place where she and I were scheduled to meet with her boss, Z Alexander.

I didn't wait to hear his response. Instead, I stalked into his office despite the protests from his secretary, ordering me to stop.

Comments like the woman's were something I'd heard most of my life, coupled with things like "Greek god" and "Adonis." And, worse, a comparison to the model whose likeness had been used for the Marvel comic book character, Ares. True, it had been the fodder used when I was given my code name. However, the initial sketches had been drawn for the release of an issue that came out twenty years before I was born.

I cleared my throat, which was unnecessary for Z, who watched me walk in and didn't bother to try masking his amusement at my hearing what the woman I was assigned to work with had to say about me.

"Good morning," I said, taking a seat in the empty chair before it was offered. "You must be Margeaux." I looked her up and down, letting my gaze linger a little too long on her ample cleavage.

While my intention had been to make her feel as ill at ease as her inappropriate comments had me, the stirring I felt in my groin was as surprising as it was unwelcome.

She folded her arms, covering her breasts, and raised her chin. Her eyes bored into mine when I finally looked up at her face. "Point taken," she muttered.

My smile was as unexpected as the rate at which my attraction to her was building. Good on her for not pretending she hadn't classified me as a piece of meat, as they say.

Z cleared his throat like I had when I walked in. "Well, this will be interesting," he muttered.

I couldn't agree more.

About the Author

USA Today best-selling author Heather Slade writes shamelessly sexy, edge-of-your seat romantic suspense.

She gave herself the gift of writing a book for her own birthday one year. Sixty-plus books later (and counting), she's having the time of her life.

The women Slade writes are self-confident, strong, with wills of their own, and hearts as big as the Colorado sky. The men are sublimely sexy, seductive alphas who rise to the challenge of capturing the sweet soul of a woman whose heart they'll hold in the palm of their hand forever. Add in a couple of neck-snapping twists and turns, a page-turning mystery, and a swoon-worthy HEA, and you'll be holding one of her books in your hands.

She loves to hear from her readers. You can contact her at heather@heatherslade.com

To keep up with her latest news and releases, please visit her website at www.heatherslade.com to sign up for her newsletter.

MORE FROM AUTHOR HEATHER SLADE

WINE COUNTRY ROMANCE

BUTLER RANCH
Kade's Worth
Brodie's Promise
Maddox's Truce
Naughton's Secret
Mercer's Vow
Kade's Return
Butler Ranch Christmas

WICKED WINEMAKERS
CENTRAL COAST
FIRST LABEL
Brix's Bid
Ridge's Release
Press' Passion
Zin's Sins
Tryst's Temptation

WICKED WINEMAKERS
CENTRAL COAST
SECOND LABEL
Beau's Beloved
Cru's Crush
Bit's Bliss
Snapper's Seduction
Kick's Kiss

WICKED WINEMAKERS
RUSSIAN RIVER VALLEY
FIRST LABEL
Bas' Blend
Hux's Harvest
Wolf's Want
Oak's Vintage
Cooper's Claim

COWBOY ROMANCE

COWBOYS OF
CRESTED BUTTE
A Cowboy Falls
A Cowboy's Dance
A Cowboy's Kiss
A Cowboy Stays
A Cowboy Wins

ROARING FORK RANCH
Roaring Fork Wrangler
Roaring Fork Roughstock
Roaring Fork Rockstar
Roaring Fork Rooker
Roaring Fork Bridger

SANGRE VISTA RANCH
Thorn's Stand
Stetson's Storm
Maverick's Reckoning
Cinch's Wager
Flints Chance